CHARLIE

ERIN O'REILLY

ALSO BY ERIN O'REILLY

Addicted to You
Spectre of Fear
Next Time
Ready for Love
Return to Me
If I Were a Boy
Through the Darkness
Deception
Fearless
'55 Ford
Fractured
That Kiss
Revelations
Wolf at the Door
Sandcastles

When Hell Meets Heaven Series
Echoes of the Past
Paradox of Love
The End Game
Requiem

With JM Dragon
Say You Won't Go
Against All Odds
Take Me as I am
Echoes of the Past
The End Game
Requiem
Earthbound
New Beginnings
Atonement

CHARLIE

ERIN O'REILLY

Affinity
Rainbow Publications

2020

Charlie
© 2020 by Erin O'Reilly

Affinity E-Book Press NZ LTD
Canterbury, New Zealand

1st Edition

ISBN: 978-1-98-858854-4

Editor: CK King, Raven's Eye Editing
Proof Editor: Alexis Smith
Design: Irish Dragon Design
Production Design: Affinity Publication Services

ACKNOWLEDGMENTS

This story would never been written without the encouragement and feedback from my dear friend, Julie. She kept me going. On the days I'd say, "I just can't do it." She considered the source and understood by saying, "Let me know when you can." And I would. Such is life on chemo drugs.

Thank you, Affinity's editing team. First is the beta editor, Nancy, who pointed out where I needed to fill the story in or out, and where I'd used the wrong names. Next, CK, the editor extraordinaire, who helped me make the story coherent and always makes me a better author by her comments. Then comes, Alexis, who proofs the story finding any errors that might remain and making sure I've added all the right information. The final story then goes to Alice, who takes one last look making sure the story is as clean as possible. Thanks to Nancy for the fantastic cover design. Thank you, Affinity Rainbow Publications for taking a chance on this story.

Of course, none of this would happen without the readers who invest their time and money to read what I write. Thank you, readers. Your feedback is what keeps me writing.

DEDICATION

For Julie

TABLE OF CONTENTS

Charlie

PRO☐OGUE

The night was balmy. A few fireflies lifted from the ground to flash and dance to the cacophony of crickets, cicadas, and the random howl of a coyote. On the wraparound porch, Hannah Garvin sat in the rocker that once belonged to her great-grandfather. It was at this time, in the dark of night, that she was acutely aware of the distinct possibility that she would be the last link of her once prominent and proud family farming in the panhandle of Texas. As she slowly rocked, the vision of her girlhood friend, Charlie, came to mind. She always did. Charlie was her one true friend, who knew her inside and out and loved her anyway. At least that was what Hannah thought until Charlie disappeared without a word. Her thoughts traversed memories of their times together.

CHAPTER ONE

The spring on the old wooden screen door moaned in protest, as Hannah used her hip to open the door. She was carrying a tray with three tall, plastic tumblers filled with ice and sweet tea.

"Here you go, Daddy and Mama, just the way you like it."

"Did you make sure it has nuff sweetnin?" Sam Garvin asked.

"Sure did. You got extra, and Mama gets her special brew...one teaspoon of sweetnin." Hannah carried her tumbler to the top porch step, where she sat leaning back against the railing. She looked out across a portion of the six hundred and forty acres of land they owned and took a long drink of her tea. "Looks like all the rest of the family have called it a night." Hannah looked at her mother. "Mama, is there anything I can do to help you with all the extra people?"

"I don't think so. I enjoy the boys and their families being here."

"Okay, but let me know if it gets to be too much."

Ada took a sip of her tea and smiled. "I don't have my foot in the grave yet, so I think I can handle them." Ada laughed.

"Thank god for that." Hannah grinned.

"It's fixin' to rain," Sam said.

"No way. That lightning is way over in New Mexico. It'll peter out before it gets to the border." Hannah gave her father a big smile.

"Mark my words, girly, it'll rain tonight and tomorrow. Might even see some water in that disappearin' lake."

Hannah put her tea down and rested her elbows on her thighs. Every time someone mentioned the disappearing lake, she got the same uneasy feeling.

"You listnin' to me, girly?"

"Sorry, Daddy, I was thinkin' of somethin' else. What did you say?"

"I said, you wanna make a bet on the rain?"

"What do I get out of it?"

"A day off."

"And you have to take Mama and me out to that Dos Rios place for supper if I win."

"Sounds like a win for me no matter what happens with the rain." Sam laughed.

†

Later that night, a clap of thunder rattled the house. Big fat drops of rain could be heard pinging on the tin roof. Hannah woke, trying to catch the fleeting tendrils of the dream she was having. She closed her eyes and recalled that someone was calling her name and waving their arms to get her attention. That was all she remembered before she fell back to sleep. A few hours later, she woke to the smell of coffee and bacon. Hannah yawned and crawled out of bed, ready to start the day.

No day off for me. I heard that rain last night. Secretly she was glad. A day off meant entertaining her sisters-in-law and the nieces and nephew. Running after small children or holding babies was not her way to spend a day of relaxing. With a yawn and a sigh, Hannah headed for the bathroom and a shower.

"Mornin'." Hannah entered the kitchen eager for breakfast.

"Good morning, sweetheart. Come, sit and join us. I just put the food on the table, so it's hot." Ada waved her over.

Bo and Mack and their families were visiting from Amarillo. The kitchen table was jam-packed with people. She nodded toward her dad. "How much rain did we get?"

"Nuff for you to lose the bet." Sam grinned.

"Yeah, yeah, I heard the rain." She leveled her gaze at him. "Shoulda known better than to bet with you, Daddy. You've been farming this land for almost forever." She laughed. "You'd know if it's gonna rain or not. How much did we get?"

"We got a little less than an inch of moisture."

"Never thought we'd get anything close to that. I swear, I thought it was nothing but heat lightning off in the distance."

Hannah scooped some scrambled eggs on her plate, along with two strips of bacon."

"Good thing you're up." Bo speared a biscuit from a bowl. "You need to go into town and pick up the order at Wilkerson's."

"Why me?"

"We helped moved the irrigation last night and you didn't," Bo said.

"We're about out of hay and straw, along with chicken feed." Sam looked at Hannah and grinned. "Besides, I need these big strong boys of mine to do some heavy liftin'."

"Hey Sis, I'll go into town with you," Mack said. She could see his eyes pleading for her to accept.

"Don't think so. Those city jobs made the two of you go all soft. You need to do some hard farm work like I do every day."

"Are you trying to shame us?" Bo asked. "The way I see it, you chose to stay here, and I didn't."

"Alrighty then, I guess you told me," Hannah countered, all the while grinding her teeth.

"Both of you stop this right now," Sam bellowed. "Let's enjoy our time together. I don't want to hear anymore bellyachin'."

"Sorry, Daddy," Bo and Hannah said in unison.

Hannah looked at the floor and slowed her breathing, while clenching and unclenching her fist. The fact that both her brothers left home to pursue jobs other than farming had been a bone of contention between them for years. As the youngest by four years, she was left at home with no choice but to take on the duty. She was the only one to stay behind and help her parents on the farm. She shook her head and grabbed a couple of biscuits, before getting up and kissing her mother. "Do you need me to pick anything up for you or do you want to go along?"

"No darlin', I'm going to Nelly's to help with the quilt she's making for her new grandson."

The phone rang and Ada answered. "Hello. Oh Nelly, I'll be there as soon as I clear the breakfast dishes... I'm sorry to hear that. Is there anything I can do to help you?" She laughed. "Okay we'll do the quilting tomorrow then. Bye for now." Ada smiled at her daughter.

"That was Nelly. She took a tumble this morning and wants to do the quilt tomorrow. Guess I'll be going to town with you after all."

"Great. I welcome the company."

"Patsy and Lucy, do you want to get the kids ready and come with us?" Ada was looking at Suzanna, Bo's seven-year-old daughter. "What about you?"

The two daughters-in-law were darting glances back and forth between the brothers as if pleading for help.

"Ah, no I don't think so," Patsy, Bo's wife, said in her heavy Texas accent. "Sammy is playing outside. He'll need a bath before he can go anywhere." She shrugged. "Sorry."

"Jess is playing in the room." Lucy rushed out of the kitchen, closely followed by Patsy.

Suzanna stood stock still. "Do you wanna go with us, sweetie?" Hannah asked.

"My daddy promised me that he'd take me for a ride on the tractor today." She took a step toward the door, then walked rapidly toward it.

"Okay. Guess that's a no. Looks like it's just you and me, Mama." Hannah smirked. "I do believe they are afraid of me."

"Oh, stop saying things like that." Ada swatted her daughter's arm gently. "I doubt they think of Morton as a town they'd go to for their kind of shopping."

"Yeah, you're probably right. The lure of the city took the farm girls out of them."

"Now you give me a few minutes to get ready, then we'll have a mother-daughter day out."

Hannah smiled and shook her head. She poured herself a cup of coffee and sat back down, sipping her coffee and biting into a biscuit she'd grabbed earlier. Her mother would have to change her clothes, do her hair, and put on lipstick before she went to town. Hannah looked down at her long-sleeved, light-blue shirt and jeans. She polished her boots on the back of her jeans leg and nodded. "I'm ready to go."

CHAPTER TWO

The pickup truck Hannah was driving rattled as it bumped down the dirt road toward town.

"Pull over," Ada said.

Hannah pulled to the side and put the gear in park. She braced herself and hoped she was wrong about what her mama wanted to see. She knew she wasn't. "Is something wrong, Mama? Did you forget something?"

"No, I'm fine." Ada rolled down her window and pointed. "Would you look at that," Ada said with wonderment in her voice. "I don't believe I've ever seen it that deep."

The sight of the disappearing lake took Hannah's breath away. She could feel the knot that always twisted her stomach, as her eyes tracked across the wide expanse of water and focused on the far side. "Charlie," she whispered.

"What was that?"

"Nothin', Mama. That's a lot of water. We'd better get going." Hannah put the truck in gear and took off down the dirt road. Despite all the rain, a plume of dust followed behind them. Thoughts of Charlie and how they'd first met at the disappearing lake permeated her mind. No one in her fourteen years had ever captured Hannah's full attention like Charlie had. Her first love. Only love. Forever love.

When the truck left the dirt road for the paved road, Ada turned to Hannah. "You're being mighty quiet. Somethin' bothering you, sweetie? You're not worryin' about the tiff you and Bo had, are you?"

"No, Mama. I'm just goin' over the list for Wilkerson's that Daddy wanted, along with the additions to his order that he told me about before we left. I don't want to forget something and have to make this trip again today. That's all. Sorry."

"No need for sorry, sweetie, I was just checking on you."

Hannah reached out and turned on the radio. "We can listen to some music." Lady Antebellum was singing "I Need You Now," and she changed the station.

"Okay. I guess I should go over my grocery list to see if I missed anything. With extra people in the house, I'll need more food."

"When are they leaving?"

"At the weekend. You always let Mack and Bo get under your skin, baby. That's why they say the things they do, to rile you." Ada reached over and squeezed Hannah's arm. "Just ignore them."

"Easier said than done." Hannah blew out a breath and nodded. Thoughts of Charlie were crawling into every crevice of her brain. *If only I could get her out of my mind.*

Try as she may, the memories of those days were never far away.

"Let's not let the boys spoil our day together."

"Okay, I'll try." Hannah gave her mother a weak smile. "Mama, I'm gonna drop the trailer off at Wilkerson's first, so we can go to the market while they load Daddy's order."

"Sounds good to me. I don't have that much to get."

"We aren't in a hurry. You can take your time and look at all the shelves." Hannah smiled. "I know how you like to shop."

"That I do, darlin', that I do."

†

The supermarket in Morton was the closest grocery by twenty miles, making it the only choice. If they wanted to go to Hereford or all the way to Amarillo it would take an extra half hour. Once inside the store, Hannah saw the huge smile on her mother's face. It wasn't often that they got to go out together and even rarer that her mama had all the time she needed for shopping. Her daddy usually drove into town, always in a hurry. He never let her just take it all in. Her mother was a true shopper, looking at everything on each shelf. Hannah dutifully followed behind, pushing the buggy and watching it fill rapidly.

"Look, Hannah, they have sardines. I've never seen them here before. I wonder what they taste like."

"Fishy."

"You're probably right about that." Ada laughed and put the tin back.

They continued shopping and soon the basket was full.

"Mama, I thought you didn't have much to get." Hannah grinned. "Good thing I brought the trailer. Let's get this loaded up and head on over to Wilkerson's."

"Did you remember the ice chest?" Ada asked, as they left the store and headed for the pickup.

"Yep." Hannah began loading the paper bags full of groceries into the bed of the pickup. Ada put all the frozen and stay-cold items in the two ice chests they'd brought. "Looks like we're ready to go to Wilkerson's. They should've had enough time to load the trailer."

"I'll just take a look around while you check on the order, sweetie," Ada said, as the two women walked into Wilkerson's.

"Don't buy out the store, Mama. Remember, you do have a reputation to live up to."

"Stop."

Ada was shaking her head, as she waved a hand in her daughter's direction and began walking around the store. Just like at the market, she loved to look and to touch everything. One time, she'd pushed a buggy around this store, picking up this and that until she realized it was full. When Sam saw it, he raised such a ruckus that a crowd soon gathered around them. From that day on, Ada never took a cart again. Even now, she could feel a blush crawling up her cheeks.

"Ada? Ada Garvin, is that you?"

She turned to see a man standing next to her. "Well I'll be, Bobby Gaines. How long has it been? How's Martha doing?"

"It's been a few years." Bobby looked away. "Martha hasn't been well ever since...well if I'm not farmin', I'm takin' care of her."

"Other than taking care of her, what do you do? I remember you liked to play forty-two at the Grange with everyone." Ada laughed. "I went there once but all the clacking of the dominoes drove me crazy."

"I don't get out much. Takin' care of Martha is a full-time job. I don't have time for dominoes."

"Has your daughter arrived back to help out?" Ada smiled. "I still remember our girls being thick as thieves and doing everything together. Then one day they weren't. I always wondered why."

"She doesn't come around much," Bobby shook his head and looked away. "To tell you the truth, after the summer she left for West Texas State, we never saw her again. She just left for college and never came back." There was sadness in his voice.

"Oh, I'm sorry to hear that, Bobby. That must be so hard on you and Martha. Do you at least know where she is?"

"From what I've heard from my cousin, who lives up near Canyon and the university, she works at an elementary school, teaching second grade."

"Who are you talking about?" Hannah came to stand by Ada.

"Charlene. You remember her, don't you? You two were best friends back in high school." Ada smiled at her daughter before noticing the stricken look on her face. "Hannah are you—"

"Mr. Gaines, it's good to see you again." Hannah held out her hand and he took it. "How have you been?"

"I'm doing okay. Still keeping the old place running. Switched to sunflowers a few years back, and that gives us enough to live on." Bobby Gaines gave Ada a look of defeat, and her heart went out to him.

"Bobby just told me that Charlene is a teacher in Canyon." Ada saw her daughter turn her head away and had a feeling that there was a story she needed to hear. "Are all the supplies in the trailer?"

"Yes ma'am, they are. We'd best be going before the cold stuff melts."

"Yes, we need to go." Ada turned to Bobby. "It was great seeing you again. Please give Martha my regards and don't be a stranger. Think about coming out to our place for a visit one day."

"Will do," Bobby said before walking away.

"Come on." Ada hooked her arm into her daughter's. "I think we need to talk."

Once back in the truck, Ada said, "Okay, spill. What was that all about?"

"Mama, there's nothin' to talk about. What was in the past stays there. It's been enough years that it's time to let go." Ada could see her daughter set her jaw and grind her teeth, which was typical of how she reacted when stressed.

"I could see the sorrow, Hannah. It is as plain as day to me, and probably Bobby could see it too. You need to tell me." Ada shook her head. "All these years, I thought we'd done something to make you so sad. I thought it was because you decided not to go to Tech, leaving you on the farm with us and not out in the world like your brothers."

"Mama, it has nothin' to do with you or the family. Will you please just let it go?"

"I don't think I can do that."

"Mama, please…let it go," Hannah said in a measured and pleading tone.

"Okay, I will stop asking. Just know that if you ever need to talk, I'll be there for you." Ada could see the pain and devastation on her daughter's face, and that made her heart cry.

"I know," Hannah said softly. "Some things are better left alone."

For the rest of the drive home, Hannah had to deal with all the memories of Charlie, skirting her every thought and trying to get in. She tried to drown them out with the radio playing loud, but that didn't help. When they drove past, she gave the disappearing lake a sideways glance. She desperately wanted to be alone so she could cry. All these years, Charlie had only been an hour and a half away. *Yet, she never contacted me.* "After all we meant to each other. Why did she leave?" she whispered.

"What was that?"

"Nothing, Mama, I was just singing along with the radio." When the farmhouse came into view, she let out an audible sigh. Once she took care of the supplies, she could go off by herself and try to figure out what to do next. She pulled the loaded pickup into the yard.

Hannah saw her father standing by the barn door.

"Okay girly, unload everything. Once you git that straw out, put it in the barn and make sure you spread it out good for the chickens. Then feed hay to Old Bessie and Bossie."

"But Daddy, why can't the boys do some of it? Hell, I went to town to get it. The least they can do is spread out the hay. It's not like it requires much in the way of brains, and it won't hurt them to do the work. They've become lazy with all that desk work they do."

"You'll not be speakin' to me that way, girly. I told you what to do. Now do it. As for your brothers, they will be goin' to bed early tonight after doin' their jobs." He gave her a wink, and there definitely was a twinkle in his eye.

Hannah knew she wouldn't win this one and unhappily walked to the trailer to start removing the straw and hay, while her mother took the groceries inside. Fortunately, Patsy and Lucy were there to help her mama. Desperate to be alone so she could deal with seeing Charlie's dad again after all these years, she picked up speed and soon had all the bales out of the trailer. She finally sorted Old Bessie, the milk cow, along with Bossie, the other cow that they would slaughter for meat. After she had straw in the eight chicken coups, Hannah walked around the back of the barn and vanished.

CHAPTER THREE

The disappearing lake looked just as it did the last time Hannah sat on the large flat rock. She'd sat on it at least a hundred times since Charlie left. Just as the water filled the depression in the ground, so did the memories of Charlie fill her mind. She'd waited for Charlie on this very rock, in the mid-morning hours, six years earlier.

They were eighteen. Charlie would be going north to West Texas State, and Hannah would go south to Texas Tech the next day. The plan was to meet at 'their' place, so they could say good-bye privately. Hannah looked at her watch— ten thirty—Charlie was an hour and a half late. Concerned that something had happened, Hannah began to walk toward the Gaines' farm, quickening her pace the closer she got. Her stomach ached and fear crept into every pore in her body. Something was going on with Charlie. She just knew it. In the four years since they'd met, Charlie had never been late for anything. The Gaines farmhouse came into view, and Hannah finally released the breath she was sure she'd been holding since she began her trek there. She walked up to the front door and knocked.

The door flung open so hard that Hannah thought it would fly off the hinges. "What do you want," Martha Gaines spat out. "Haven't you done enough damage? What more do you want from us?" she screamed.

Charlie had said that her mother often went into a rage and screamed at everyone. Hannah assumed that this was just one of those occasions.

"Get away from my door, sinner."

"Mrs. Gaines," Hannah said softly. "Remember me, I'm Hannah Garvin and I'm a friend of Charlie. Is she here?"

"You hedonist bitch. Leave my daughter alone and stop teaching her to be a degenerate. Now get off my property and never come back."

"I…I just wanted to tell her good-bye." Hannah held both of her hands up facing toward the enraged woman. "That's all."

Mrs. Gaines reached for something by the door.

The rifle pointed at her made Hannah gasp. "Okay, I'll leave. Please tell Charlie I was here and to please send me her address at school."

"I'll tell her no such thing. Now git out, or I swear I'll strike you down dead."

With slow and deliberate moves, Hannah turned away and slogged toward the road. The crack of gun fire, followed by a bullet hitting the dirt in front of her, had Hannah covering her head with her arms and running for her life.

Tears dribbled down Hannah's cheeks. She threw a few pebbles into the water before standing. She lifted the hem of her shirt and swiped at her eyes and face. There was no way she'd go home looking like she'd been crying for hours. Mack and Bo would tease her, and her mama would fuss over like a mother hen. No, she would not let any of that happen.

The breathing exercises a doctor taught her after her appendix surgery always helped relax her. They'd clear her mind of Charlie for a short time. After twenty minutes, she felt calm embrace her and knew that she could go home. No one would know she'd been crying. Hannah looked at her wristwatch. Time to get a move on. Being late for supper was a big no-no in the Garvin house.

†

Just as Hannah reached for the handle on the screen door, Bo appeared from inside the house and pushed the door open.

"Well, well look who we have here. Where have you been, Sis? We looked all over for you."

The familiar gleam in his eye told Hannah he wanted to start something with her.

Not today. She grinned at him. "All my chores were done, so I thought I'd take a walk." She brushed past him and went into the kitchen. Supper smelled delicious.

"Good, you're back," Ada said. "We're almost ready for supper. Patsy and Lucy helped with dinner, and I have some new recipes."

"Mama, what about Daddy? You know he only likes his meat, potatoes, gravy, and biscuits for supper."

"Not to worry, sweetie, I've got that covered. Trust me, he will never know." Ada gave Hannah a wink, then a slight hug. "Hannah is finally here. Let's all sit down."

Hannah sat in her usual chair and looked around the kitchen. Her mother was in her glory, scurrying about the room handing dishes to her daughters-in-law. At fifty-five, she was just as active and strong as Lucy and Patsy. At times, she could outwork even her sons.

Sam came stomping into the kitchen. "I'm hungreee." He looked at the family gathered there before taking off his hat and sitting at the head of the table.

Hannah smiled when she saw her daddy's red hair standing straight out of the back of his head. *Ball caps, you gotta love 'em.* She fondly looked around the table at her brothers. Varying shades of red hair on all the siblings signified that they all belonged to the strong man who sat at the head of the table.

"Just sit yourself down, Sam, and be patient. It'll get on the table when it gets there," Ada said. "Or if you want, you can help bring the bowls to the table."

"Naw, I'll just sit." Sam grinned and winked at his wife. "I'll let you gals do the woman work."

The looks on Lucy and Patsy's faces were priceless. Hannah knew her daddy was pulling their chain and reveling in their reaction. More times than not, he would set the table and help out in the kitchen.

"You know he's joking, right?" Hannah asked her sisters-in-law. They both shook their heads and continued helping.

Once all the food was on the table and everyone was sitting, they held hands and recited grace. "Bless us, oh Lord, and thank you for the bounty you provided us. Amen."

Everyone immediately began to pass plates of chicken fried steak, mashed potatoes, fried okra, hominy, milk gravy, and biscuits.

"I thought you said you made something new," Hannah whispered to her mother.

"I did." Ada grinned. "Those aren't mashed potatoes but cauliflower."

"Oh. To be honest I thought the texture was a bit off."

"If I add enough butter and salt, your daddy wouldn't know the difference."

Hannah let out a small laugh and shook her head. "You aren't going to do this again, are you?"

"No, darlin', just trying to keep the girls happy."

"Thank goodness."

"Who's ready for some fried pies and ice cream for dessert?" Ada asked. Everyone nodded. "Give me a hand will you, Hannah? Patsy, can you and Lucy clear the table?"

†

Later that night, Hannah sat in the front porch rocker, going over the day's events. Seeing Charlie's dad had taken her by surprise. The emotions brought forth were soul deep. After her encounter with Charlie's mother, Hannah had tried to find her. She'd driven to WTU with Charlie's picture in hand. She'd asked everyone around the campus if they knew her. About to give up, she finally found someone who had seen her moving into one of the dorms. Hannah ran all the way to the building. She knocked on every door but found no further information and dejectedly walked to her truck.

The letter she wrote to Charlene Gaines c/o West Texas State University was her last option.

Dear Charlie,
What happened? Why did you leave so abruptly without a word? I miss you so much. I think of you every waking moment, and you are in my dreams. Please, write me back and let me know that you are okay. I love you so much. My heart is aching to see you again.
Hannah

She'd expected to hear from Charlie soon after that. Nothing came. She reasoned that since she hadn't received the letter back marked *return to sender* it had been received. Two months later, her heart filled with joy when she collected the mail and saw a letter addressed to her from Charlie. Hannah tore open the envelope and unfolded the paper. It said...

Hannah, never contact me again. Charlene

That mail irrevocably broke her heart. It was the last time that she heard from her one true love. Now the ghost of a love that was warm and beautiful, tender and alive, was all that she had left.

CHAPTER □ OUR

The cotton seeds had germinated, and the tiny plants were peeking out of the rich soil. Hannah walked the fields, making sure that all the rows were producing plants. They would worry about the weather and insect infestations for the next six months, until all the cotton was harvested. Hannah kicked a rock and watched it dribble down the path in front of her. When she came upon it again, she began to kick at it but stopped. The rock looked exactly like a half of a heart. Her mind immediately went to the first day she met Charlie.

The rain had fallen hard over two days, and the disappearing lake was full. At fourteen, it was Hannah's responsibility to post *no trespassing* signs. Kids would flock to the 'lake' and frolic in the water. There was always the threat of someone getting injured or drowning. Money was tight, and the last thing her folks needed was a lawsuit because someone got hurt on their property. Hannah walked across a field and past the rust garden that was home to all the discarded vehicles and machinery. When she arrived, she saw that about a dozen kids were splashing and laughing in the water.

"Ugh, what do I do now?" She stapled a few signs on the fence posts near her and began to move closer to the water to tell them to go home. She knew all the kids. If she told them to get off their land, there would be repercussions at school the next day. Her eyes diverted to a girl she'd never seen before, sitting alone on a big rock by the water. "I wonder who she is." Hannah walked toward the girl with tentative steps. The closer she got, the more she could see just how pretty the girl was. Finally there, she sucked in a deep breath and smiled.

"Hi, I'm Hannah Garvin. I don't think I've seen you around these parts before."

"Just moved into the old Parker place with my folks and my brother, Bobby Junior." The girl grinned. "I'm Charlene Gaines, but everyone calls me Charlie."

"Pleased to meet you, Charlie. Mind if I sit?" Hannah pointed to the large rock the new girl was sitting on.

"No, not at all. My brother dragged me down here, otherwise my mom wouldn't let him go out with his new friends. I think she wanted to get rid of us. He's almost three years older than me and doesn't need a babysitter." She pointed to a short, round boy standing in the crowd of kids. "That's Bobby Junior trying to look taller." Charlie laughed. "He got Mom's short genes, and I got Dad's tall ones."

For a moment Hannah thought of her own family. Her mother was the shortest at five foot eight. Her daddy was six four, both her brothers were six two, and she was five ten. "How old is your brother?"

"He's going to be sixteen."

"He might still get taller."

"He might, but I'm not holding my breath, and I don't think he is either." Charlie grinned. "I'll be starting school on Monday."

"Will you be going to Three Junctions?"

"Yeah, I think that's the name. It sounded weird to me. Why did they give it a name like that? Aren't they usually called by some president's name or a hero or a street?"

"Well, the school is located where three counties meet." Hannah shrugged and looked away. She didn't know why it was that all she wanted to do was sit there and talk to the new girl all afternoon. Just then, she heard a booming voice that she recognized.

"You kids get your butts over here."

"Darn it," Hannah whispered.

"What's wrong?"

"I was supposed to put up no trespassing signs." Hannah looked at the three lone signs and was glad she got them up at least.

"Okay, do you mind tellin' me why you boys ignored the signs?" Sam pointed to the few Hannah put up. "You're on my property."

All the boys looked down at their feet.

"Well, sir, it is hot today, and we don't get much of a chance to get in water like this," Lucas Bowman said.

A softening came over her dad's face, and Hannah could see a sparkle in his eyes.

"We're having a lot of fun," Doug Eckhart said.

"Now you boys do know that I graze my cows out here, don't you?" Sam grinned when some of them nodded. "I do believe that you fellas are playin' in their bathroom. By now you got all the patties smushed up just fine." Sam readjusted his Stetson work hat and nodded. "You all go ahead and play in the water. I hope none of you get sick from it 'specially if you swallow some of that water." He laughed before he turned away from the gaping boys.

"Did you see the look on all their faces when my dad told them they were playing in cow shit? I think they may add to the poop." Hannah laughed along with Charlie.

"Wonder which one will be the first to leave?"

"It'll probably be that little guy over there. Robbie Maddox is the youngest one."

"Your dad has a wicked sense of humor. Do cows really do their business there?"

"Yep."

"Come on, girly, we got work to do," Sam bellowed from right behind her.

Hannah looked at her father. Where had he come from? "Can you give me another ten minutes, Daddy?"

"No. You're burnin' daylight sittin' there on your butt. Come on now." He looked at Charlie. "I haven't seen you 'round these parts. Who are you?"

"I'm Charlene Gaines. We just moved here."

"That's right. The old Parker place. I heard some guys at the Grange talkin' that your family moved in there."

"Yes, sir. Pleased to meet you, Mr. Garvin."

"Hannah you can see your friend another time. Let's go." Sam tipped his hat to Charlie and began to walk away. "Come on, girly, get a move on."

"I need to go."

"I can tell. Maybe I'll see you at school."

"No worries on that." Hannah got up. "The school is not that big." She laughed, then reached into her pocket. She held out a nugget of rose quartz to Charlie. "Here, this is for you." Hannah watched Charlie's fingers wrap around the rock before a smile curved her lips. "Gotta go." Hannah took off running to catch up with her father.

†

A scan of the classroom on Monday morning brought Hannah's gaze to the big smile on Charlie's face. The smile was for her, of that she was sure. She hurried over to her new friend.

"Hey," Charlie said. "Is this your class too?"

"Yep. I…I didn't think you'd be here, since you weren't on the bus."

"My dad brought us so he could register us. I'll be taking the bus home this afternoon."

"Really? Wanna sit with me?"

"Of course."

Mesmerized, Hannah zoned out from everything else around her.

"Hannah, did you hear me?" Geneva Weston asked.

Hannah shook her head. "What? Oh hi, Geneva. What did you say?"

"I asked, who's your new little friend?" Geneva's eyes fixed on Charlie.

"This is Charlene, her family moved into the old Parker place." Hannah turned and smiled at Charlie. "This is Geneva Weston. She's in our class."

"Hi," Charlie said, just as Mrs. Albright walked into the room.

"Everyone take your seats." Mrs. Albright waited for the room to quiet. "We have a new classmate, Charlene Gaines. Charlene, why don't you take the empty desk behind Hannah? Raise your hand so she knows who you are, Hannah."

"Yes, ma'am," Charlie and Hannah said in unison.

Hannah could see Charlie never took her eyes off the waving hand as she walked toward her.

"Is this the right seat?" she whispered.

"Yes."

Charlie grinned and sat down.

That afternoon, after getting her blue and gold school jacket out of her locker, Hannah met Charlie at the door and walked with her to the bus. She nodded to the back, and they sat together in the last row.

"Hey, Hannah, you always sit with me. What gives?" Geneva was standing beside them.

"I decided to sit with Charlene today…show her the ropes."

"Yeah right." Geneva stomped away.

"I didn't mean to get in the way," Charlie said shakily. "I can change seats."

"No." Hannah spoke sharper than she meant to. "Geneva is a hanger on. Two months ago, it was all about Billy Bradly, then it was me. Tomorrow it will be someone else."

"Poor girl. We should make an effort to be nice to her."

"I've done that." Hannah said. "That will only make her think we want to be her best friends. Believe me, we don't want to do that." Hannah winked.

"Oh."

The bus rumbled down the road. At each stop, Hannah let Charlie know who got off and where they lived. "Your stop is the next one."

"Will the driver leave me off at my road? Does he know he has a new student? I'm not exactly sure where I am."

"Burt, that's our driver, knows who you are and where your stop is." Hannah looked around the bus. "Where's your brother?"

"My dad picked him up early for a dentist appointment.

"Oh. Why don't I walk you to your farm? That way you won't get lost."

"Will the bus wait for you?"

"No."

"That's a long walk to your home."

"Not far."

The bus stopped and Hannah stood. "Come on, I'll walk you home."

"I'd like that."

"Hannah, it's not your stop," Burt said.

"I know. I'm walking my new friend home." Hannah could see the confused look of the driver. His eyes darted between them.

"Well, next time I need to have a note from your parents."

"Yes, sir." Giggling, Hannah and Charlie got off the bus and headed down the dirt road.

From that day on, Hannah walked Charlie home each day, before she walked across fields of cotton to her own house.

Hannah blew the memory off with a deep sigh. She tucked the half heart rock in her pocket and kept on walking. The fields were free of weeds, and for that she was happy. Hoeing weeds was the one job she hated the most. In the distance, she could see her mama hanging out laundry. Her daddy was pruning apple trees. She loved life on the farm. Most days were slow and easy. Others were fraught with worry about weather. Would this be the year that would break them and cause the family to lose their farm? All it took was one sand or hailstorm to wipe it all away. Her eyes tracked over the flat landscape with nonexistent humidity and winds that blew relentlessly. How she wished she had someone other than her parents to share it all with.

Charlie would have been perfect.

CHAPTER ☐ IVE

"This looks good, Daddy." They stood in a field of irrigated cotton.

"Been two weeks since we got any moisture. That dryland cotton ain't gonna make it if we don't get some soon."

"Hey, you gotta think positive. Isn't that what you're always tellin' me?" Hannah saw him nod slightly. "I remember it being this dry in the past. We always harvested a good crop from the dry land and got a top price. Why is this year any different?"

"It ain't. That wireworm scare we had last month got to me. I realized I'm not as young as I used to be." Sam looked at his daughter. "If it weren't for you bein' here, I woulda given up years ago."

Hannah studied her father. She hadn't noticed that he was a bit pale and thinner. His face bore deeper wrinkles. She realized he was getting older and sighed inwardly. "Don't think like that, Daddy. We'll get through this just fine. Look at it this way, at least the wind isn't blowin' too hard today." Hannah grinned.

"That's one way of thinkin' about it." Sam shook his head. "Sure glad you decided to stay here with us instead of goin' off to school and leavin' the farm behind like your brothers did."

"I'm still here, Daddy, and I won't leave you and Mama here alone."

The truth was that Hannah hadn't wanted to be there. Obligation kept her there more than anything. As her parents grew older, she could see that if their farm was to continue to flourish, she needed to stay. The plan had always been that she'd go off to college with Charlie. They'd room together and maybe build a future. They were both accepted at Texas Tech, and their plan was starting to take shape. Then, Charlie got a scholarship to West Texas State and everything changed. Though disappointed, Hannah understood why Charlie had to take advantage of the scholarship opportunity. Although the plans for being together changed, their bond had remained unbreakable. Charlie left for college without saying good-bye, and that bond broke.

Hannah kicked at the sandy soil, as a memory of their first summer together took hold.

School was finally over, and they spent every day together. Hannah rose early. She fed the chickens and gather their eggs, milked the cows and let them out to graze. She made sure they all had fresh straw or hay, then she'd sit on the front porch and wait. The first glimpse of Charlie coming down the road always caused a warm, happy feeling to wash over her.

"Hey." Hannah could feel her body heat. "I'm glad you're here. I have a basket for a picnic." She held up the basket and took a tentative step down the stairs. "That is, if you'd like to have a picnic with me."

"Of course I would, silly. Where are we going?" With a wide grin, Charlie winked at her friend.

"Well, I was thinkin' maybe on that rock by the disappearin' lake. You know, the one where we first met."

"Our place it is," Charlie said brightly and grabbed Hannah's hand. "Let's go. What do you have in that basket?"

"Hmm, not sure. Mama fixed it for me."

An hour later they both were sighing with contentment.

"That was the best picnic ever." Charlie lay on the blanket, rubbing her tummy. "Let's do this all the time. Your mom is the best cook. I especially liked the brownies. Will you thank her for me?" Charlie rambled. "I can only remember going on a picnic with my family one time."

"Really? This is only your second picnic? You never just spread out a blanket and ate lunch in your yard?"

"No. My mother is a germaphobe, among other things." Charlie frowned. "She'd be mortified if she saw me eating out in a cow pasture."

"Oh, I'm sorry, I didn't know."

"Nothing to be sorry about. That's her, not me. If it wasn't that it would be something else. Why do you think I don't invite you to my house? My mom is...well...strange. I wish she was more like yours." Charlie fixed her with an intense gaze. "I don't care what she thinks. I am having a great time and can't wait to have another picnic with you."

"And you will." Hannah smiled. "I am so glad we became friends." She could feel the well of happiness growing inside her. Hannah had never met anyone like Charlie.

"Do you have a boyfriend?" Charlie asked.

"God, no! Boys are all obnoxious and full of themselves."

"Do you think that opinion will change at some point?" Charlie knitted her eyebrows.

"No," Hannah said seriously. "What about you? Have you met any guy here that you like?"

"I'm not really interested in any of them. I want to concentrate on getting some sort of scholarship so I can move away."

Stricken, Hannah bowed her head. "Oh," she said softly.

"Silly girl. We're going together. I won't go away to school unless you go with me." Charlie moved next to Hannah and took her hand. "You know that don't you?"

"I do now."

Charlie's smile widened. They sat there holding hands, until Hannah heard the big bell. Her mother used that bell to call her, Mack, and Bo home.

"I've got to go. Mama will keep ringing the bell until we all are standing next to her."

"Will I see you tomorrow?"

"Absolutely."

"It's a date then." Charlie leaned in and gave a quick kiss to Hannah's cheek.

There were only a handful of days they didn't spend together that summer, and the new school year was the same.

That year found them doing everything together. Even though Charlie didn't like basketball, she joined the school's girls' team so they could play together. In return, Hannah joined the spirit club with Charlie and helped plan school events.

The time had cemented their friendship forever. They became inseparable, or so Hannah thought. Hannah shook off the memory as she stood in a cotton field with her daddy. She pointed her chin toward the southwest. "Looks like we might be gettin' some rain soon."

"Let's hope so, girly. Like I told you, we're close to losin' the dryland plantin'. If we don't get some moisture soon, we will be in a world of hurt."

"Did you hear that?" Hannah's ears picked up on the sound of thunder in the distance. "Do you want to make a bet?"

Sam shook his head. "Don't think so, girly. It's a sure thing it'll rain today." He put his arm around Hannah's shoulders. "I'm thinkin' I'll take you and your mama out to dinner Saturday night." He grinned. "My girls deserve a night out." He readjusted his hat. "Come on, let's get inside. It's almost supper time, and your mama's gonna ring that bell soon."

Sam, Ada, and Hannah sat on the porch after supper, drinking sweet tea.

"Sure is nice out here after how hot it was today," Ada said.

Lightning flashed in the distance, and the wind picked up.

"Looks like we'll get some moisture after all," Sam said.

"That storm came up quickly," Hannah replied. "I swear I looked out there a minute ago, and that earlier storm had passed us by."

"We'd better keep an eye on it." Sam stood and went to the porch railing. He squinted at the approaching storm. "We got some time left before it gets here."

"Can I get either of you anything? There's some cobbler left."

"Not for me, Mama, I'm still full of the supper I ate."

"I'd take some of that cobbler with a scoop of vanilla ice cream," Sam said.

"You sure?" Ada looked at her daughter. "Peach cobbler is your favorite."

Hannah rubbed her belly. "No, I'm good."

Ada went into the house, and five minutes later she rushed out onto the porch. "There's a tornado warning for us. They spotted one near the school. We need to get in the shelter."

They abandoned the porch and hurried behind Ada into the house. The back corner of the root cellar was deemed the safest area and Ada's designated spot, since she was the smallest. Hannah stood in the middle of the small room, and Sam stood halfway up the stairs, ready to hold the door closed if needed.

While she listened to the wind and the rain that pelted the tin roof, Hannah closed her eyes and prayed that their crop would be spared. If she opened her eyes knew what she'd see—Charlie. The memory of being alone in the cellar with Charlie flashed in her mind.

The day was hot, hotter than usual for the last days of May. Her parents had left for Amarillo to see their doctors and do some shopping at a 'real' grocery. They'd also visit Mack and Bo, who'd moved away to the city. School had ended five days earlier, and Hannah was relishing the idea of spending the summer with Charlie. She was on her way over, and the thought of spending the day without anyone else around was exciting on so many fronts. Hannah looked up at the clear blue sky and sighed. Life was indeed good.

Breath got caught in Hannah's throat. Charlie drifted down the dirt road in skinny jeans. *Kiss Me* beneath the red lips on her t-shirt sparked an invasion in Hanna's body that she hadn't felt before. There was a tightness between her legs. The slight cramping made her wonder if she'd started her period.

"Shit. Not today."

The closer Charlie got, the more intense the feeling became. She found that her underwear felt damp. Charlie stopped and looked up at her from the bottom of the steps. That was Hannah's undoing. She tried to hold her breath against the strange feeling that swept over and caused her underwear to become wetter. She was almost panting.

"Are you okay?" Charlie asked, concern clear in her eyes.

"Not sure. I think my period started."

"I doubt that. We have the same cycle, and that was two weeks ago."

"Come on in." Hannah waved her hand. "I'll just check."

Charlie followed her into the house then touched her hand. "I'm going to get a glass of water."

"Go ahead. You know where the glasses are. I'll be right back."

Hannah collected clean underwear from her bedroom and went into the bathroom. She sat on the toilet after pulling the shorts and underwear off, fully expecting to see blood. What she found was only wet underwear. "Huh." When she wiped herself with toilet paper, the strange feeling came roaring back. She moved her fingers, and the eruption of pleasure she felt was unlike anything she'd ever experienced. She jumped at a knock on the door. Guilty, she withdrew her fingers and flushed the toilet.

"Hannah, are you okay? Do you need any help?"

"Ah...yeah...I'm good. Let me wash my hands, and I'll be right there."

"Okay, if you're sure you're all right."

"I'm good."

A few minutes later, when she saw Charlie sitting at the kitchen table, the feeling returned. Hannah wondered if she were sick or something.

"Hey, what are we gonna do today? I was thinking we could lay out in the sun or have a picnic." She frowned at Hannah. "Is everything okay? Do you want me to go home?" The confusion and sadness in her voice was obvious.

"The last thing I want is for you to leave, Charlie. I've been lookin' forward to this day since we planned it."

"Me too. So why do I get the feeling something is wrong?"

"Nothin' is wrong." Hannah scratched her forehead and looked at the floor, refusing to make eye contact. "I just had a really weird thing happen, and I don't know what to make of it."

"Come on." Charlie took Hannah's hand. "You can tell me all about it." She led the way to the couch, where they sat close together. "Out with it."

"You're going to think I'm crazy."

"I doubt that. Please tell me."

"Well, I was watching you come up the road, and I got this feeling like my period was starting, even though I knew it wasn't that time of the month. The closer you got, the more I felt. When I went to the bathroom, I found my period hadn't started, but my underwear was really wet."

"Really? Hmm."

"That's not all."

"There's more?"

"Yes." Hannah couldn't look Charlie in the eye. "When I went to wipe myself, the feeling came again. It was so intense. Then I came into the kitchen and saw you, and it tried to start again." She shook her head. "I think I may have cancer or something."

Charlie let out a belly laugh.

"What? What's so funny?"

"Were you paying any attention in that sex ed class we had?"

"Not really. When you live on a farm, you know how babies are made."

"Well they talked about more than getting pregnant." Charlie moved closer, if that was possible, and lifted Hannah's chin. "You were experiencing arousal."

"Really? Like sexual?" Hannah's eyes grew wide, and suddenly, a lightbulb went off in her head. She could feel her face heat and looked away.

"Hey, it is normal and not something to be ashamed of."

"Um...I don't..."

"Hannah look at me."

Hannah raised her head.

"I've experienced it too."

"You have? When?"

The weather radio pierced the air, before a robotic voice announced a tornado warning was issued for their area. Hannah looked out the window. The sky had turned black and green. She turned to look at Charlie and could see the terror in her eyes. "Your first one away from home?" Charlie nodded. "Come on, we'll be safe in the shelter." She took Charlie's hand and led her to the trap door and safety.

"Better now?" Hannah noticed that once she turned on a light Charlie calmed down.

"Yes. I'm sorry I freaked out."

"Charlie, look at me. Which is worse…being scared of a tornado that could kill you or…thinking that an orgasm means you have cancer? Seriously."

Charlie laughed. "You've got a point." There was a loud bang, as something hit the tin roof and she jumped. "What was that?"

"Don't be afraid. I've got you and won't let anything happen to you." Hannah pulled Charlie close and kissed her forehead.

"I trust you, Hannah. You're the only one that I do."

"Don't you trust your parents?"

"No. My mom is weird, and my dad just stands there and does nothing about it or goes outside to escape."

A crack of lightning had Hannah pulling Charlie closer. When she pulled away, their eyes met. Shyly and hesitantly, their lips touched. Their first kiss kindled an explosion of feelings that Hannah knew would be forever.

Forever was a myth.

CHAPTER □ IX

"I need you to run to town and pick up the Wilkerson order, girly."

"I'm running low on canning jars. Will you pick me up two boxes?" Ada was busying herself with breakfast cleanup.

"When will it be ready, Daddy?" Hannah asked.

"When you get there. Before you go, we need to check on the dryland cotton. Buzz told me he found boll weevils in his field next to ours. Buzz has already sprayed his and we'll need to do the same if we find them."

"Come on then, let's check it out." Hannah grabbed her ball cap and the truck keys.

The weevils were eating their way through the cotton bolls. She and her daddy ran the tractor pulling the big tank of insecticide on a trailer. The long booms sprayed all the affected cotton.

Going to town for the second time that week wasn't what she wanted to do. She had no choice since her daddy had to clean up the equipment. She'd rather go to town.

"I'll treat myself to a milkshake at Maudie's." An uninvited vision of sharing a malted with Charlie invaded her thoughts. She turned the volume of the radio up, effectively erasing the memory.

†

Wilkerson's was busy. Hannah had to wait longer than usual for them to load the trailer. She wandered around the store and was surprised to see Bobby Gaines again. Her stomach roiled, as it always did when thoughts of Charlie found their way into her head and heart. Hadn't she, a short time earlier, wiped Charlie from her mind? Hannah changed her path but wasn't fast enough.

"Hannah, is that you?" Bobby called out.

"Yes, nice to see you, Mr. Gaines."

Silence ensued.

"How is Charlie doing?"

A sad look came over the man's face. "To tell you the truth, I don't know."

This was her chance to find out everything, and she swallowed hard "It's gonna take a while for my order to get done. Would you like to go over to Maudie's and have a cup of coffee with me?"

"Yes, yes I would. I don't get much of a chance to socialize." Bobby's face gentled. "Lead the way."

The small café was practically empty at midafternoon. They sat at a table for two in the corner. After their drinks arrived, Hannah was softly tapping the table and trying to get the courage to ask what she wanted to know.

"Have you heard from Charlie?" Bobby asked tentatively.

Hannah shook her head. "No," she sucked in a breath and continued. "We had made plans for how we'd see each other while in different schools. Then, without a word, she was gone."

"I remember." Bobby had a distant look on his face. "It was the day before we were to leave for school. I came in from chopping some weeds in the garden, and Charlie had her bags and all the things she wanted to take packed and in the back of my truck. I asked her what was going on. She just looked at me and walked away. I asked Martha if she knew what was happening, and she shook her head telling me that she didn't know."

Hannah could see the sadness in the man's face. "I talked to her early that morning. She was happy and excited. She told me she couldn't wait to start school. When I called her later to figure out what we'd be doing that night, Mrs. Gaines told me she couldn't come to the phone." Hannah blew out a breath. "You told me before that she was teaching so you must have talked to her at some point."

"Oh, we hear from her on birthdays and at Christmas, but that's all. It's always a very brief conversation." Bobby shook his head and swiped at his eyes. "When she first got to school, she told us never to call her. I tried once, but there was no answer. A few years later, she called us out of the blue and said she'd changed her number."

"Do you have that phone number?"

"No, she always called us, and there's just *unknown number* on the display.

"You know, I did go to your house that day. Mrs. Gaines told me to leave at gunpoint. She even shot at me."

"What? I can't believe that."

"It's the truth, Mr. Gaines." Hannah shrugged. "I never went back to your farm again."

"If that is how Martha treated you, I'm sorry. My wife has some problems that she is working out. Hannah, you were never anything but kind to our daughter."

"Do you know where she is?" Hannah pressed.

"The last I heard she was in Canyon, but that's been years ago."

"Do you know if she's married? Does she have kids?" She needed the answers but really didn't want to hear them.

"Not that I know of. Early on, I asked if she had any beaus. She told me, 'my one true love is gone thanks to her.' I never asked again."

"Who is the her? Is it me?"

"No idea. To be honest, I was so shocked by her words I was speechless." Bobby swiped at his tear-filled eyes. "I should have pressed her harder or gone to see her. I didn't, and I will regret that for the rest of my life."

Hannah reached out and squeezed Bobby's hand. "She'll come around." Tears continued to fill his eyes, and she suddenly felt uncomfortable. She looked out the window and saw that the trailer was filled and ready to go. "I need to get going, Mr. Gaines. We have weevils and my daddy needs me." She slid her chair back and stood. "Thank you."

"You'll let me know if you hear from her, won't you?" Bobby asked.

"Of course." Hannah left with thoughts of Charlie filling every corner of her mind. *My one true love is gone thanks to her* resonated the loudest, causing her to remember the day they'd pledged their love.

It was their junior year. Hannah and Charlie were closer than ever. The spirit club was preparing for the annual fall festival. The day before the event, they had to stay late. Hannah didn't mind. Extra time to spend with Charlie was a bonus in her book. They walked to the cafeteria holding hands, until they saw the principal, Mr. Boronia, coming their way. They moved apart slightly.

"Is everything ready for the festival?" Mr. Boronia asked.

"Yes, sir, everything is ready," Charlie answered. "We never had anything like this in my last school."

"You're a fine addition to our school, Charlene." The principal nodded at them before continuing toward the office.

"He didn't seem to have a problem with us holding hands." Hannah took Charlie's hand again.

"Maybe he didn't see us."

"Oh, I doubt that. He's been the principal since I was in first grade. He's pretty sharp."

Charlie pulled her into the bathroom, then stood with her back to the door. "Come here," she whispered.

Hannah knew she couldn't deny Charlie anything. Their slow and tender kiss was full of love and promise. Just as Hannah began to intensify the kiss, someone pushed against the door.

Hannah hurried over to the sink and began to wash her hands. Charlie moved away from the door.

"Sorry, I didn't realize I was leaning against the door. I'm waiting for pokey over there to finish up. Come on in,"

Charlie said to one of their classmates. "Have they started decorating yet?"

"Just about ready," Regina answered.

"Okay, we will see you there in a few." Charlie smiled at the girl, who headed to a stall.

Hannah put her arm around Charlie's shoulders and kissed her cheek before they left the bathroom and began walking toward the cafeteria.

†

The night of the Fall Festival was balmy. Farmers were waiting for the cotton to mature, and the school was open to everyone in the community to enjoy the celebration of nearing the end of a successful season. The gymnasium was crowded. Hannah kept hold of Charlie's hand, as they maneuvered through the crowd in search of her family.

"Can you believe the turnout this year?" Ada asked when they approached. "You girls did an amazing job."

When her mother gazed in the direction of their joined hands, Hannah let go.

"We had a homecoming bonfire at my old school but nothing like this. It was so much fun planning. I can't wait for the next event." Charlie bounced slightly, looking over the heads. "Look at all these people, and I need to go to the bathroom."

Hannah laughed and took her hand. "Come on, I'll get you through the crowd." She looked at her parents. "I'll meet you by the refreshments in a few minutes."

"See you there." Ada patted Hannah's arm. "Don't get lost."

The bathroom had a line. Charlie and Hannah passed it by and went to the cafeteria.

"Good thing they let the committee have access. That tea went right through me." Charlie headed for the lone bathroom that was thankfully empty.

"Oh, you really had to go. I thought you just wanted to get me alone." Hannah grinned.

"I want that too. Give me a few minutes, and I'll be all yours."

Soon, they were wrapped in each other's arms. Soft, simmering kisses grew to breathless intensity.

Charlie pulled back and smiled. "You know, one of these days we are going to have to take this to another level." She blew out a breath. "What you do to me, Hannah Garvin." She nuzzled in and kissed Hannah's neck. "I want more."

Hannah put a finger under Charlie's chin and lifted her head, before kissing her gently again. She broke the kiss and held dark eyes captive, as she raised her hand to cup Charlie's breast. "Is this what you want?" she whispered.

"Yes, and more." Charlie caressed Hannah's hand before she mirrored the action. "I want to make love with you and only you."

"As I do with you." They kissed deeply, but Hannah pulled away. "Not now. We need to get back."

"I don't like it, but you're right. Besides, I don't want our first time in some dark bathroom. I want you in my bed." Charlie blew out a breath. "That was intense."

"Yes, it was." Hannah whispered.

"Know this to be true. You are my one true love and always will be. Never forget that."

Hannah hadn't forgotten, but Charlie apparently had.

CHAPTER □ EVEN

Winter blew in on strong, frigid winds. The temperature dropped from forty-one to thirteen in a matter of hours. Hannah leaned into the wind, as she walked from the house to the barn. Bessie was huddled in a corner. Their new meat cow, Susie, huddled close to her. Neither came in her direction, as she used a pitchfork to clean out the manure. Over the whistling wind, Hannah could hear her mother calling in a desperate tone. From the barn door, she could see her mother standing in the kitchen doorway. She dashed toward the house.

"What happened? Has something happened to Daddy?" The cold air fogged Hannah's heavy breaths.

"He took a tumble. I think he's broken his arm."

"Did you call for an ambulance?" Hannah stepped inside the warm kitchen.

"He didn't want one."

"It doesn't matter what he wants. If he needs an ambulance, then we'll get him one."

Sam was sitting on the front room floor.

"Daddy, what happened?"

"That darn throw rug got tangled in my feet, and down I went."

"Are you hurt anywhere?"

"I hurt my arm. Come and look at it, girly."

After she shrugged out of her coat, Hannah gently took her father's arm. She didn't see anything that indicated it was broken. "It doesn't look broken, but you should get an x-ray." Hannah looked at her mother. "What do you think, Mama?"

"I think we have a doctor look at it, just to be sure."

"I don't need to see a doctor," Sam bellowed. "What I need is a hand to get me up off this floor."

"I'll get you up," Hannah said. "But I think we'll take you to the doctor to be on the safe side."

Sam held out his injured arm and wiggled all his fingers. He made a fist and shook his hand. "See, it's fine. I'm not gonna spend money on a useless trip to the doctor. Now get me up."

Hannah shook her head. "Have it your way." She helped him into a crouching position, then squatted behind him. With an arm under each of his armpits and the help of her mother, she lifted him to a standing position.

"Do you want some ice on your arm?" Ada asked.

"No. I'm good."

His stubbornness was frustrating. She'd quietly taken over some of his jobs as he slowed down over the last year, but he'd never admit to a thing. He had spent most of his life farming. She'd actually mentioned retirement last Spring; that tirade lasted a while. Some people were hard to help. Her mind drifted to her senior year and another difficult situation.

The Saturday before Christmas was a frosty morning. Sam and Ada had gone to Amarillo to see their new grandchild. Hannah didn't expect the knock on the door. "Who could that be at this time of the morning?" She opened the door and was surprised to find Charlie shivering and crying.

"Charlie, what's the matter?" Hannah drew her into her arms. "You're shivering. Come in and get warm." She led Charlie to a seat on the couch and wrapped her in a blanket. She sat beside Charlie and held her close. "Tell me," she whispered. "Let me help you."

"You can't."

"Let me decide that. Now please, tell me."

"My mother is having one of her episodes. It's been like five years since she had one. Now my dad tells me that it's my duty to take care of her. If I'm not at school, I have to be at the house and be her nurse. I'm not a nurse. I'm a kid," she cried.

"What about your dad or brother? Why can't either of them take care of her too? After all, it's winter and there isn't much your dad can do outside."

"He said he'd be with her all day while I'm in school, and he would need a break. I screamed at him, asking why Bobby can't help too. He said Bobby has a job and can't just leave." Charlie began to cry. "I'm seventeen, and I want to—"

"Shh, we will figure it out." Hannah pulled the sobbing Charlie closer. "Tell me, how long do the episodes last?"

"Months! I was at her beck and call for months." Charlie let out a small growl. "I don't want to take care of her. This really sucks. I want to spend time with you and not be a nursemaid. It's not like she's grateful. She isn't. She's just mean. She lays in her bed, ringing her little bell to command me to do anything she wants."

"How can I help?" Hannah kissed her cheek. "Just tell me what you need, and I'll do all I can to make it happen."

"That's just it, Hannah, my dad told me I couldn't have anyone else in the house or talk on the phone. He said it would upset her more. I told him he could get me a cell phone, then she wouldn't hear the ringing. He said, and I quote, 'Out of the question. You need to be with her at all times, without any distractions.'" She squeezed Hannah's hand. "I want to be with you. I want to spend some of Christmas Day with you." Charlie blew out a breath. "I have an amazing gift for you, Hannah."

Charlie shook her head. "I don't see how I can get out of this. We've already been accepted at Tech, so I can't say I have to stay after school to boost my grades so I can get accepted to college."

"Charlie, I know you are upset by this, but at the same time, you need to remember she is your mother. She gave birth to you. While you were growing up, she took care of you."

"I know. I sound like a petulant child, don't I?"

"Yeah, you do. Listen, we'll work something out. I'm not sure what it will be but...." a plan started to take shape in Hannah's mind. "Hey, where will your dad be when you get home from school?"

"Um I don't know. Working in the barn maybe. Why?"

"Well, if I get off the bus and walk you home like always, you could find out if he's going anywhere. If he is, then we could—"

"Spend time together."

"Exactly. We need to make the most of the time we have, and this will work. One thing though."

"What?"

"Your mother is sick. Even though it's mental rather than physical, she still needs you." Hannah shrugged there was no way she'd abandon her mother in time of need. "I know it seems to you that she's doing this on purpose—"

"Sometimes I think she is. I've had to deal with this all my life, and I'm tired of doing it."

"Next year, we'll be in school away from here. Can you hold out until then?"

"As long as I have you, I can."

Hannah pulled Charlie close and they kissed. "What is your mother's diagnosis?"

"Paranoid schizophrenia."

"That's a tough one. I had an aunt with that, and it was difficult for the family. I can only imagine what you and your dad are going through. What's going on with Bobby?"

"He's working in Dallas. His wife is having a baby that's due in a few months, so he can't help out. That's enough talk about my mother. I'd rather know when your folks will get back."

"Later tonight."

Charlie grinned. "Why don't we take this to somewhere more comfortable?"

"Bedroom?"

Charlie nodded.

Hannah stood and pulled Charlie up into her arms. "We will make the most of the time we have. You know, it's not the quantity but the quality."

Frenzied fingers undid buttons and lowered zippers. Bras were removed. Inside, Hannah shook with worry about what was about to happen. "Charlie, what do we do next? I haven't a clue."

"I think we lay down and get to know each other's bodies and what makes us feel good."

Hannah took Charlie's hand and led her to the bed. After turning down the covers, she asked shyly, "Will you join me?"

Charlie lay down and patted the mattress. "Come on, lay here next to me."

Hannah swallowed hard and crawled in next to Charlie. "I—"

Charlie put a finger over Hannah's lips. "Let's just explore." She rubbed her palm over a hard nipple. "Do you like this?"

"Oh, yes." Hannah mirrored all of Charlie's moves, as they began their exploration. They gently caressed each other's bodies. The need for more grew exponentially. Fingers found the way to their saturated centers and began to slide in and out. Although clumsy in how they pleasured each other, the result was mind blowing for Hannah. She could see that Charlie felt the same.

Lying close in each other's arms, Hannah kissed Charlie's forehead. "That was amazing."

"I never imagined I would feel this way." Charlie ran a finger down Hannah's naked body. "Can we do it again?"

"Your wish is my command." Hannah rolled Charlie over, before leaning in and taking a nipple in her mouth.

Charlie moaned and held Hannah's head. "God, Hannah, please don't stop."

"Never."

A rattling noise woke Hannah. She listened intently and realized her parents were home. "Shit. Charlie, wake up and get dressed. They're home."

"Who?" a blurry eyed Charlie asked.

"Mama and Daddy. Hurry." They scrambled to pull on shirts and jeans. Hannah pointed to underwear and a bra left on the floor. "Get those." She saw her new lover kick them under the bed.

Hannah smoothed out the blankets and sat cross legged on the bed. Charlie sat in an old beanbag. Both were reading when the knock came on the door.

"Hannah, are you asleep?" Ada asked softly.

"No, Mama, come on in. Charlie and I are studying."

The door swung open and Ada smiled at them. "Did you think we'd never come home?"

"I knew you would eventually. How is the baby?" Hannah asked.

"She's beautiful. It looks like she's going to have red hair too."

"What's her name?" Charlie asked.

"Suzanna. Isn't that a beautiful name?"

"Yes, it is. Now that you're here, I can take Charlie home."

"Why doesn't she stay? It's getting late. I'll call your dad and tell him."

"I wish I could, Mrs. Garvin," Charlie said. "My mom is under the weather, and I told my dad I'd come home."

"Oh dear," Ada said. "Is there anything I can do for your mother?"

"I'm not sure. I'll pass your offer on to my dad, and I'm sure he will let you know."

Ada nodded then smiled. "You'd better get her home then, Hannah. The truck is all warm for you."

When they arrived at the Gaines' house, Hannah saw the curtain in the main room flick.

"Did you see that?" Charlie said. "My dad probably isn't too happy with me being gone so long."

Hannah nodded. "Guess that means I can't kiss you good-bye." Hannah took Charlie's hand and gave it a slight squeeze. She pulled out a bag from the back seat. "This is your Christmas present. I think you can use it sooner rather than later." With a slight lift of one shoulder, she handed the bag to Charlie and watched as she opened it.

"Oh, Hannah, a cell phone! What a wonderful gift. I can't believe you got this for me." She gushed before leaning over and giving Hannah a quick hug.

"It's all set up. You just need to touch the *1*, and we can talk."

Charlie fingered the phone and smiled. "You are the best."

"We will always be in contact. If you ever need me, I will be there for you."

"I want to be with you always, Hannah. I promise you that I will never let you go," Charlie whispered before she opened the truck door.

In the end, Charlie forgot her promise and tossed Hannah aside like the gift-wrap from a Christmas present.

CHAPTER EIGHT

Spring rolled around and everything on the farm was in high gear. The fields were plowed, and planting day was drawing near. Sam was a proud man, completely dedicated to running the farm with all the intensity he could muster. Her father had been working on one of the tractors. At sixty-six, he worked as hard as a man half his age. She couldn't remember a day that he took off for sickness or anything else, really.

"Hey, girly, can you run into town and see if Wilkerson's has this part?" He held out his black greasy hand. "If you can't find it there, try Akins. I saw they had a tractor like ours out in their salvage lot."

"Sure. I'll check with Mama to see if she needs anythin'."

"Good idea. Ask her to bring me out some tea."

Hannah nodded and left for the house, then turned back to her father. "Anythin' else?"

"Another set of hands would be good."

"I'll be back as soon as I can." It was only a matter of time before the majority of responsibility for running the farm would be hers. She trembled at the thought.

"What does he want?" Ada asked with a grin. "You don't ever come in during the day unless he wants something. Tea?"

"You got it in one." Hannah laughed. "Mama, do you need anythin' from town or want to go with me?"

"Can't think of anything. I got most of what I needed when we went to Silverton last week."

"Okay. I'll be back by supper."

"Be careful."

Hannah accepted the good-bye kiss on her cheek.

†

Wilkerson's, as Hannah expected, was very busy. She made her way to the counter and leaned back against it, as she waited for assistance.

"What can I do for you?" a soft female voice asked.

Hannah turned to the woman and smiled. "You're new here." Black hair framed olive skin. The dark eyed woman took Hannah's breath away for a moment.

"Yep, just started last week. What can I get ya?"

"Um," Hannah shook her head before unwrapping the greasy rag that held the part. "Do you have this part by any chance?"

"Let's see what you have." Hands with long fingers picked up the part, and the woman gave it a cursory look. "We should. Let me go check."

"Thanks." Hannah watched the woman walk away and was surprised at her body's reaction. Tingles of pleasure that she hadn't felt in a very long time ran through her body, as she watched the woman walk away. After less than five minutes, the woman came back.

"We have it, but we'll have to move boxes out of the way. The guys are gonna get it. Shouldn't be too long."

"Not a problem." Hannah eyed the woman. "You're new around these parts, aren't you?"

"Yep, been here a week or so."

"What brought you here? It's not like this town is on anyone's bucket list." Hannah grinned and held out her hand. "I'm Hannah Garvin, welcome to our little piece of Texas." The young woman gave her hand a firm shake.

"Thanks. I'm Mick. As to why I landed here, I inherited my grandpa's house, here in town."

"Really. What was his name?"

"Tom Hendricks."

"I knew him. He passed a few weeks ago, didn't he? I don't remember seeing you at his funeral. They did remark that your grandpa had several grandchildren."

"I wasn't there." Mick shrugged. "I didn't have enough money for even a bus ticket, so it took more time than I thought it would to hitchhike here. All I could do then was visit his grave. Grandpa was the only one who really cared about me, and I will miss him." She smiled. "What's your story, Hannah Garvin?"

"Not much really. I've lived and worked here all my life. I'm living with my parents on our cotton farm right now."

"How noble of you."

"The last thing I am is noble" Hannah didn't like Mick's demeaning tone. There was something disconcerting about the woman, but she couldn't put a finger on what it was. There was no doubt that she was attracted to her. That thought stirred something she hadn't felt in a long time that bubbled deep inside wanting out. *Ridiculous.*

"Anyone who stays on the farm is noble, in my book," Mick said, jarring Hannah out of what she was thinking.

"Here you go." Greg, one of the store's workers, placed the boxed part on the counter. "Oh, hey Hannah."

"Hi, Greg. Thanks for getting this for me."

"Yea thanks, Greg." Mick smiled at him, and Hannah saw Greg blush.

"And, here you go." Mick lifted the box to Hannah. "Do you want this on your account?"

"Yes." Hannah knew she had to get back, but for some reason was reluctant to do so. She wanted to stay and talk with Mick more. "Do you have some time to go to Maudie's for coffee or a bite to eat?"

Mick raised a finger and made a circular motion. "Twirl around for me."

Hannah frowned. "I'm not doing that." She looked around. "I know everyone here." Mick's eyes were raking over her body. Hard as she tried to deny the impulse, Hannah's body responded.

"Fair enough. Meet me at Maudie's tomorrow at one, Hannah. I'll buy lunch."

"I'll be there." With a smile, Hannah took the tractor part and walked away. She hadn't felt this happy in a very long time. She grimaced. "What will I tell Daddy? He won't be happy if I leave for the afternoon."

†

Hannah arrived at Maudie's early and sat in the far corner, watching the door. The lunch crowd had thinned, and she was glad of that. *Is this a date? It certainly seems like a date.* The idea made her excited. She hadn't had a date since Charlie. She looked up and saw Mick walk through the door, and all thoughts of the past were pushed to the background.

"Hi." Mick slid into a chair next to Hannah.

"Hi." Hannah suddenly felt awkward and looked away.

"Is everything okay?" Mick asked in a concerned voice.

"It's all good...um...I'm just not used to having a lunch date." Hannah could feel her face heat up. "In fact, this is the first one in a very long time."

"You're kidding me, right?"

"Afraid not. The farm keeps me pretty busy. There's not a lot of free time."

"You're gorgeous. I can't believe they aren't knocking your door down." Mick shook her head.

Hannah could feel her face heat. "Why would you think that? This is a small town. Everyone knows everyone, and we all went to the same school. Trust me, no one ever said I was gorgeous."

"That's amazing. You have that beautiful cinnamon hair and dark-blue eyes that a lover could easily get lost in. Add to that your magnificent, lean body and you, Hannah, are the complete package of what anyone would want."

"Okay." Hannah figured all the words were a way of luring her into bed. *Not yet.*

"You've never had a special someone?"

"I did have someone in high school." Hannah looked at Mick, hoping she wouldn't see the despair she knew would be there. "It didn't work out."

"Good. That leaves the field wide open for me." Mick grinned. "Yesterday must have been my lucky day."

"What can I get ya?" Maudie looked at Hannah. "You want the BLT with a tea like always?"

"Yes."

"And you, dear?"

"I'll have the same, a BLT," Mick answered.

"Anything to drink?" Maudie asked.

"A Diet Coke," Mick answered.

"We only have Pepsi."

"I'll have tea then." Mick turned her full attention back on Hannah. "Guess you're a regular."

"It's either here or Rosie's. There is a DQ a few miles out of town. Like I said, it's a small town, and everyone knows everyone."

"So, tell me what you would rather be than a farmer?"

Hannah shrugged. "Not sure. I was accepted to Tech, but in the end I didn't go."

"Why? I'd think you'd have jumped at the chance to go. What were you going to study?"

"Not sure. For a long time, I thought I wanted to be a vet, but that would cost too much and take too long."

"You never went for it, did you?

Hannah shook her head.

"Why not?"

"I didn't have a reason to go anymore, and the farm was familiar and safe."

"What reason?"

This was not the conversation Hannah wanted to have with Mick, and she refused to have it. This was her chance to move on and leave Charlie in the past. "Enough about me. Did you always want to work in a hardware and feed store?"

Mick grinned. "Sure, working at Wilkerson's has been my life's dream. One day, I will be in charge of the store."

"Lofty goals. You do know that Fred Wilkerson has two sons who work at the store, don't you?"

Mick laughed. "Actually, my plan was to fix up my grandpa's house and sell it. Then I guess I'll see how I feel about moving on, or maybe I'll decide to stay here."

"And make a career of working at Wilkerson's? Somehow I think there is more to this story."

"As there is to yours." Mick winked. "When we know each other better, we can tell all our secrets."

"Here ya go." Maudie set the plates with the sandwiches and chips in front of them. "Tea for you, Hannah, and your friend. Let me know if you need anything else."

"Thanks, Maudie."

Conversation took a back seat to eating. Hannah looked at Mick. She wanted to know more about the woman and get to know her better. At the same time, to share information about her relationship with Charlie with a relative stranger seemed like a betrayal.

"Wow would you look at the time?" Mick nodded toward the clock on the wall. "Sadly, I've gotta go. Give me your phone?"

"Why?"

"You'll see."

Hannah handed over her phone. Mick entered something, then held the phone out and took a selfie. She tapped a few more times. When she handed the phone back, the picture she'd taken was showing. "Now you'll know it is me when I call."

"Yes, I definitely will." Hannah laughed. "Thanks for lunch. Next time it's on me."

"So there'll be a next time?"

"Absolutely. You are someone I'd like to get to know, Mick."

"That feeling is mutual. I'll see you later. Bye for now."

That night, for the first time in longer than she could remember, Hannah lay in her bed and did not think of Charlie. Instead she wondered when she'd meet up with Mick again.

CHAPTER NINE

Three days passed, and Mick invaded Hannah's mind more and more. She didn't have the courage to call. It was more important to have a physical connection when they talked. All that she needed to do now was to find an excuse to go to town.

"Hey, Mama, if you're goin' for groceries today, do you want some company?"

Ada lifted her head from washing the dishes with a startled look. "There are a few things I need, but I wasn't planning on going today."

"This is the first day of the limited sale at Wilkerson's, and there are a few things I've had my eye on. I want to get them before they run out. I thought we could kill two birds with one stone, if you wanted to go too."

"Okay, I'd love to have you along." Ada wiped her hand on her apron. "Give me a few minutes to get my purse. You're driving, right?"

"Of course I'm drivin'."

"What's goin' on?" Sam asked when he came into the kitchen. "Sounds like you two are makin' plans."

"We're goin' into town, Daddy. Mama needs to pick up a few things from the grocery store, and I want to check out the sales at Wilkerson's."

"Do I need to go along?" Sam asked. "Might see some stuff I need."

Hannah unconsciously balled one hand. Her plan to have some time with Mick was getting all mucked up. "What have I started...a damn circus?" she whispered.

"What did you say?" Sam asked.

"Can we just go to town and not make a circus of it?"

Sam scratched his stubbled cheek. "Don't see no reason for me to go and spend money on somethin' I don't really need. If you see some fine-grain sandpaper, pick me some up."

"Will do. Now that's settled, when do you want to leave, Mama?"

"Just give me a few minutes and I'll be ready."

"I'll have the truck all warmed up and ready for you. Thanks." Hannah grabbed the truck keys and left the kitchen. "Shoulda just gone by myself," she mumbled.

†

Hannah pulled the old truck up in front of the Morton Grocery and looked at her mother. "I'll be back in a little while," she said.

"What? You're not goin' in with me? There are things I want to look for at Wilkerson's too."

"I know, Mama. I just don't want to miss out gettin' what I wanted."

"What's the matter? Do you have ants in your pants? I won't be long, Hannah, so just relax. I'm sure they won't sell out in the next thirty minutes."

"You're right. Why don't you go on inside? I'll park, then be with you," Hannah watched her mother walk into the store and sighed. All she wanted to do was find Mick and ask her out to dinner. Hopefully, her mother wouldn't be following her all around the store. She got out of the truck feeling ashamed for resenting her mother being there. "What is the matter with me?" she mumbled. "Calling Mick would have been a lot easier than this rigmarole."

Hannah walked into the grocery store and found her mother puzzling over which bananas to buy. "The yellow ones are the best."

"Oh you." Ada swatted at Hannah's arm. "I don't want to get any that are too yellow or have bruises. One day, you'll have to do the buying, and you won't have a clue."

"I will have a clue, Mama, because I pay attention to how you buy food."

"We'll see how much you've learned. Go pick us a nice head of lettuce."

Hannah walked over and lifted a head of lettuce in each palm. She returned and handed a head to her mom. "The heavier the better, right?"

"You have been listening. Good girl." Ada smiled.

Once they'd finished with the groceries and had them loaded into the truck, they headed for Wilkerson's Dry Goods.

"Look, they have canning jars on sale." Ada pointed to a sign in the window. "I know I'm going to need more eventually."

"Didn't I buy you several boxes not too long ago?"

"You can never have enough." Ada began pulling a shopping basket out of the line. It wouldn't budge. She tried again and got the same result.

"Here let me help," Hannah said. "There's a trick to this." She jiggled the basket, lifted it slightly, and out it came.

"Thank you, Hannah, you are a treasure. I'll come find you when I'm done in the kitchenware."

"Well that means I have about an hour or so." Hannah smiled broadly.

"No, it doesn't," Ada said indignantly.

"Mama, you'll get over there and before you know it, you'll be in a conversation with someone. You do know everyone." Hannah gave her a pointed look and grinned.

"Go find your Daddy's sandpaper. I'll find you later."

Hannah walked rapidly around the store, hoping to see Mick. No luck. She wasn't there. Her heart plummeted. *Might as well get the sandpaper.*

"Hello, beautiful, I was hoping you'd come in here again."

A warm feeling made Hannah smile and she turned. "Me too. That's why I came in here today." She took a step closer to the dark-haired beauty with a curvaceous body, who was already standing next to her. "I was wondering if you'd like to have supper with me tomorrow evening."

Mick shook her head. "I'm sorry I can't."

"Oh." Crestfallen, Hannah took a step back. "Okay, I need to get—"

"Wait." Mick reached out and took Hannah's hand. "I didn't say I don't want to have supper with you. I just can't tomorrow night. I have a guy coming by the house to give me an estimate on what the renovation will cost."

"You know," Hannah said. "I swing a mean hammer and would be happy to help you get the house ready to live in. Just let me know when. I'll be there." *Unless Daddy needs me.* Hannah raised her shoulders at the thought.

"Really? That'd be great. Not sure my bank account will be enough to pay a professional for what I'll need."

Hannah looked at Mick in question, wondering why she couldn't afford a bus ticket but had a bank account. "Mick, I thought—"

"There you are, dear." Her mother appeared next to her. "Who's your friend?"

"Hi, Mrs. Garvin, I'm Mick Hendricks." She held out her hand.

"Any relation to Tom Hendricks?"

"Yes, ma'am, he was my grandfather."

"I'm sorry for your loss. Tom was always a good man, who was willing to help everyone."

"Thank you. Well, I'd better get back to work. Can I help either of you find anything?"

"No, I found what I was looking for." Hannah held up the sandpaper. "You ready to go, Mama?"

"Yes. I need to go to Farmer's to get some new towels. They don't have the ones I like here."

"This is the shopping day for the Garvin family. It's a long drive so we need to get things while we're in town." With a discrete wave good-bye, Hannah steered her mother toward the checkout with an arm around her shoulder.

The truck left a dusty trail as it rumbled down the dirt road to the farm. Hannah was thinking of Mick and thought she'd call her and set up a time to meet.

"So, tell me about you and this Mick."

"What?" Hannah frowned in confusion and frustration at being dragged from her pleasant thoughts.

"Are you and her an item?"

"An item?" Hannah stole a quick look at her mother. "What are you getting at? She's a new friend. That's all."

"You know, for a lot of years, I watched you and Charlie. I could see the love and devotion you had for each other. When she left, I worried about you all the time. You were so sad and devastated." Ada reached over and touched her daughter's arm. "I knew you were a couple. It was obvious."

"Mama, I don't want to talk about it." Her eyes remained focused on the road ahead while trying to tamp down the astonishing revelation from her mother. "Do you hate me or think I'm evil or unnatural?"

"No, I don't. Love is love, Hannah. When you find it, you have to grab it."

"Not everyone thinks like you, Mama."

"That's their problem, not yours. The way I see it, you are happy again, and I now know why. Her name is Mick."

"Mama, please let me see how this goes before you label us a couple."

"Fair enough."

Just as Hannah turned the steering wheel to the house, she saw her dad and swallowed hard. "Does Daddy know about me and Charlie?"

"He never mentioned anything to me. I think he would have." Ada reached over and patted Hannah's leg. "Not to worry. If he doesn't like it, he'll come around. You are his girly, after all." She smiled. "And I've got your back. Just know that I will keep this between us, sweetheart. It isn't my story to tell."

"Thanks, Mama, I love you." Hannah let out a breath.

"As I love you, sweetie."

"Okay, we'd better get the food you bought into the house." Hannah chuckled. "Did I ever tell you how much I love to grocery shop with you?"

"No. I always thought you went with me because your daddy told you to."

"Nope. I go because I want to."

The strong hug around Hannah's shoulders was evidence of her mom's love. "I like you being there with me. Come on, let's get busy with these bags."

Hannah jumped out of the truck. The weight she'd been carrying on her shoulders since Charlie left lifted a little.

CHAPTER TEN

"I'm going to town tonight," Hannah announced, before getting up from the table and taking her dishes to the sink. "Mama, do you want help with the dishes before I go?"

"What I want to know is why you're goin'. Can't remember the last time you went into town at night. Wasn't that for that square dance at church?" Sam held a hand to his forehead. "You got a beau?"

"Do you still have a headache?" Ada asked.

"Yes," Sam answered. Hannah knew her father was having headaches for the last few days and was in a cantankerous mood. When he looked at her, she cringed slightly knowing there'd be an inquisition.

Like a dog with a bone. "Why are you goin' to town at night, girly? Who's your friend? Do I know him?'

"I'm helpin' a friend work on a house that needs renovation, Daddy."

"Who? I don't recall you ever goin' into town at night, alone." Sam squinted and held his tea glass to his forehead. "Damn headache."

"Sam," Ada said, "it's Tom Hendricks' granddaughter. I met her the other day. She's a lovely girl."

"Well, it would have been nice if someone told me," Sam bristled.

Ada turned to Hannah. "Don't stay out too long and call me before you head home."

Hannah laughed. "Ever the mother hen, Mama. I'll call." When she got to the door, she whispered, "He needs to have someone check out those headaches, Mama."

"I know. The problem is getting him to agree."

"Stubborn."

"Yes, he is. Now go."

†

Hannah stood on the sidewalk looking at Mick's house. The exterior was the typical stucco that every other home in the area had and was in need of a paint job. She saw several places where the plaster was gone and would need repairing. The soffits, at least the ones she could see on the front of the home, all needed replacing. The tiny front yard was filled with rocks. A lone tree, clinging to life, was in need of an arborist. She walked up to the smallish porch noting a gaping hole in a corner. With her balled hand, she hesitantly knocked on the screen door. Flecks of green paint fell off. Hannah could hear footfalls coming toward the door.

"Hey, you're here. Come on in." Mick greeted her with a broad smile on her face.

The front room Hannah walked into was compact, dwarfed by a giant, flat-screen TV on one wall. She thought that Mick's grandpa must have been a smoker, since the walls had a yellow tinge in desperate need of a painting.

"Well this is it," Mick waved her hand around. "As you can see, it needs work."

"From what I've seen, a little paint will go a long way to make it better."

"That's what I thought when I first came in." Mick pointed to her right. "There are two bedrooms and a bath over there. The biggest disasters are next." She walked into the kitchen. "See what I mean?"

What little linoleum was left looked like it hadn't been washed in years. "I see what you mean. What condition are the appliances in?"

"I scrubbed them when I first moved in. For the time being, they're okay. Come on, there's more."

They stepped out into what could only be called an add-on. A high-end washer and dryer stack faced a tall cupboard that was used as a pantry.

"I think this room has promise." Hannah looked out the door window. "Does that garage belong to you?"

Mick shook her head. "Yep." She sighed. "You won't believe what it looks like. Come on, I'll show you."

Mick struggled to open the door. When it finally gave way, Hannah looked inside. Her jaw dropped. "I remember your grandpa being a collector. Everything in here is probably an antique."

"You think this looks like someone's collection? I think it looks like he was a hoarder."

Hannah stepped into the jam-packed garage and picked up an oil lamp. "Hoarders don't save something like this or keep everything neat like this." She saw at least ten more oil lamps and several wooden wall phones. "Look around, Mick. Everything is grouped together. I imagine you can get a great deal of money out of this collection."

"You really think so?"

"Yes." Hannah noticed a gleam in Mick's eyes. "You really didn't know what all this was?"

"Not a clue." Mick rubbed her face and looked away. "I opened the door and saw it chock full of stuff that reaches the ceiling in some places, and I closed the door."

Something seemed off. Mick wouldn't meet Hannah's gaze. *Is she telling the truth?* Anyone in their right mind would have at least gone inside the garage to see what was there. *Right?* Mick told her that she didn't have enough money for a bus ticket to get to Morton. *Wouldn't she be on the lookout for something worth money in her grandpa's house?* Hannah spent years going to yard sales with her grandmother, looking for exactly what was in that garage. The contents were a treasure trove.

"Hey, let's go have a cold beer and figure out what to do first." Mick's voice brought Hannah out of her musing.

"Sounds good." She followed Mick and shook her head. She was being foolish. There were plenty of people who wouldn't realize the worth of the antiques in the garage. *Wouldn't they?* "We should check through all the books in the house, Mick. People always put money in them."

"I already did that and found a twenty. At the time, I didn't have a job, so it came in handy. I could eat."

"How long before you started at Wilkerson's?"

"About a week. Mr. Wilkerson remembered me from when I visited my grandpa and hired me on the spot." She looked around the room. "I think we should do the interior first." Mick took a swig of her beer. "If you're right, maybe I can sell enough stuff from the garage to pay for getting the house painted."

"From the little I saw, Mick, and I'm not an expert by any means, I think you can get enough to paint and put a new roof on."

"Will you help me go through all of it and identify the good stuff?"

"Sure, but I think you might want to get the inside done first. You never know what you might find tucked away in some hidey-hole. Often, people stash money in an old coffee can or catchall. I even heard of a man and his wife who hid thousands of dollars in mason jars and buried them in the back yard."

"That sounds like something grandpa would have done." Mick laughed. "I'll buy the paint tomorrow. What color do you think for the walls?"

"The fixer-up shows on TV say grey is the 'in' color right now. But, since you will be living here, it should be a color you like."

"I like grey." Mick held out her empty bottle. "Want another beer?"

"No thanks. I need to head on home. I had a big day fixing one of the tractors with my dad." Hannah got up off the couch.

"Oh," Mick said with a disappointed voice. She moved closer. With hands on Hannah's hips, Mick pulled her close and kissed her softly.

Hannah didn't know how to react. Yes, she was attracted to Mick, but they'd just met. She didn't know how old Mick was or who her parents were. Why did her grandpa leave everything to her and not someone else in her family? *Does she even have a family?* She took a step back, effectively breaking the kiss.

"Did I do something wrong?" Mick asked. "I thought we were on the same page here." Mick attempted to grab her again, and Hannah moved away.

"We are. It's just too soon for me. I want to get to know you, Mick, before I commit in that way."

"What's so important that you need to know about me?" Mick asked angrily, before turning away.

"That's it then? You just turn away and not give me an answer?" When she had no reply, Hannah picked up the tool bag she'd brought and walked to the door, all the while hoping that Mick would tell her to stay. She didn't.

Once in her truck, she looked back at the house and saw Mick watching from the door. "I don't have time for games." She slammed her palm on the steering wheel, before starting the engine and heading for home.

There was no way she would let anyone into her heart, especially not as easily as Mick seemed to think. Her effortless escalation to anger worried Hannah. She'd given her heart away once and would not easily let it happen again, even if it meant she was destined to spend the rest of her life alone. Before she'd commit, she needed to know all about Mick. She recalled Mick saying she might move away and shook her head. "No way will I get involved with her if she's not staying around."

†

Hannah quietly climbed the porch stairs. With her hand on the screen door handle, she said a silent prayer that it wouldn't complain with a squeal. It didn't comply. She opened the front door and was surprised to see her mother sitting alone, reading a magazine.

"You're early. I thought you were going to call."

Hannah looked at her feet. "Sorry, Mama, I forgot."

"What's wrong'" Ada asked. "Didn't it go well?"

"Where's Daddy?" Hannah was desperate to change the discussion.

"His headache went away, so he decided to go play forty-two at the cotton gin." Ada patted the cushion next to her on the couch. "Sit."

Hannah complied and let out a prolonged sigh.

"Everything okay?"

"I misunderstood why she wanted me to go there. I thought we'd get to work. Instead, she just showed me around, and we discussed what needs to be done."

"What's that then?"

"The house needs paint inside and out, along with a new roof. The linoleum in the kitchen is all torn up."

"So, are you going to help her?"

Hannah shrugged. "Not sure yet." With a questioning look she asked, "Was Mr. Hendricks a collector of antiques?"

"He owned the This and That Antique Shop in Overton. Why do you ask?"

"There's a garage with the house. It's filled with antiques like Granny used to look for. He had ten old oil lamps that I could see, and an old writing desk that I'd buy if it were for sale."

Ada patted her daughter's arm. "What's wrong?"

"Nothing." There was no way she was going to let her mother know what had happened with Mick.

"Not buying that. Come on give."

"We were there looking around at all the stuff, then we had a beer and talked about what to do first. Next thing I knew, she had her arms around me and kissed me. When I objected, she got mad, and I left. End of story."

"She didn't hurt you, did she?"

"No, Mama. No need for alarm. It wasn't like that."

"I thought you liked Mick."

"I do and I'd like to get to know her better."

"But?"

"I'm not sure. There is something about her that I just can't figure out."

"The best way to solve that, sweetheart, is to get to know her better."

"That's what I'm trying to do, Mama."

"Then what's the problem?" Ada frowned.

"I've spoken to her twice at the dry goods store and we once had lunch at Maudie's. It just doesn't seem like I know her enough to take it to…um…the physical part yet."

"Okay, I'm confused. I thought you said you only kissed. Was there more than that?"

"No," Hannah said indignantly. "It took two years before Char—"

"There we have it," Ada said.

"What?"

"Charlie."

"This had nothing to do with her!"

"Are you sure?"

"Yes. She's in the past. Remember, she walked away not me." Hannah stood and began to leave just as the front door opened,

Sam looked at his wife, then his daughter. "What's goin' on?"

"Nothing, Daddy. I was just on my way to bed." Hannah kissed her dad's cheek and whispered, "See you in the morning. I'll be ready to do some plowing." Hannah quickly walked away and heard her dad say, "What's that all about?"

Hannah closed her bedroom door and flopped down on her bed. She took out her phone and saw she had two missed calls and one voice message, along with five text messages. All were from Mick. The voice message was simple. "Hannah, I'm sorry. Can we start over? Please. Call me." The text messages had a similar tone, and she wondered if walking away had been the right move. *Was Mama right?* Was her reaction because of Charlie and not Mick?

She picked up her phone and sent a text message to Mick.

I need to work on the farm for the next few days. We can meet for lunch when I get done, if you want. She pressed send.

It was a few seconds later that she had a reply. *Perfect. Just let me know when.*

There are times in life when one must let go of the past and start living in the present. At that moment, she thought Mick might be the one she would move forward with.

CHAPTER ELEVEN

Tired and dirty, Hannah and her dad walked into the kitchen.

"Well I'm glad that's over with." Sam stretched and groaned. "My back is tellin' me I'm gettin' too old to sit on a tractor plowin' for four days."

Hannah snatched a biscuit from a plate on the table. "Think I'll eat then hit the sack." She rolled her shoulders. "I'm gettin' too old too." She grinned. "Now can I take a day or two off, Daddy?"

"I'm thinkin' we both deserve a rest, but there's still work to do."

"Come on you two. Supper is getting cold." Ada pulled out her chair and sat at the table.

Hannah and her father sat down, and they said grace.

"I told you about my friend, Mick. I said I'd help her fix up her grandpa's house. I need to take some days off to do that."

"Family wins over friends. I need you here," Sam said.

"You know, I've worked the farm all my life and never once have I asked for time off."

"I need you here, girly. There's work to be done."

"We both know that for the next week you will be at the Grange playing forty-two." Hannah could feel her heart pound as she flexed her hand.

"I need you here. End of conversation," Sam bellowed.

Hannah glared at her dad, as she got up from the table and started to leave.

"Hannah," her father said softly. "I'm sorry. I haven't been feelin' too good. I shouldn't take that out on you."

"What's wrong?" Ada asked. "Have the headaches gotten worse?"

"No. I just feel worn out, and my neck and shoulders are hurtin' from sittin' on the tractor for so long."

Hannah walked over to her dad and put a hand on his shoulder. "You need time off, Daddy. The tractors and the farm will still be here while you rest. When you're ready, we'll do our work." Hannah looked directly into his eyes. "Think about seein' a doctor. He could give you somethin' for your shoulders and take a look at why you have the headaches."

Sam patted her hand. "You're right, girly. I'll think about doin' that. You go help your new friend."

"Thank you." Hannah kissed her dad's cheek and headed to her room.

A long hot shower would help her unwind. She was still obsessing over her dad forbidding her to help Mick. "It's not like I get a salary," she mumbled into the water. She recalled the one time she'd mentioned that to her dad. He told her, "You got a bed, a roof over your head, and three squares. What more can you want?" Fortunately, her granny gave her a trust fund that she could get money from if she needed.

Hannah's thoughts turned to Mick, while she soaped her body. When she stepped out of the shower, she'd come to decision. It was time to take her life back. She had mourned the loss of Charlie for almost six years. "It's time to let go." She'd call Mick and arrange to have lunch with her, the first serious step toward moving on with her life. She picked up her phone and dialed. "Hey Mick, it's Hannah."

The next morning Hannah sat at the table eating breakfast. "Mama, where's Daddy?"

"He was up most of the night, going to the bathroom, so he's sleeping in."

"Sounds like he has the flu or somethin'. He should get it checked out. The sooner the better."

Ada laughed. "First, I'd have to convince him that he needs to do that. In all the years we've been married, I have never been able to convince him of much. Just like always, he'll go when he's ready."

"Yeah, that sounds about right. Well, I'm off. If you need anythin', just call and I'll come back." She called back over her shoulder, "Oh, and don't let him go out and work today."

"I'll try."

†

Hannah appreciated the view, when Mick pushed open the door to Rosie's Cantina. Spectacular was the word that came to mind. She could swear her heart stopped for a moment. Mick had on skinny jeans, a tight t-shirt, and boots. Her black hair was braided, and her overall look was casual but sexy.

"Sorry I'm late," Mick said. "Old man Scott came into the store and was trying to hook me up with his grandson." Mick laughed. "I finally had to tell him that I was taken, or I'd probably still be there."

"He's done the same thing to me. I went to school with Mitchell. He's a nice guy, but I was never interested in him."

"Because you already had someone?"

"Yes." Hannah frowned when tears pooled in her eyes. How was she ever going to move on if people kept reminding her of the past?

"Hey, I'm sorry if I said something wrong." Mick reached across the table and took her hand.

"You didn't," Hannah said more brusquely than she intended. "It's in the past, and I've moved on."

"I'm glad." Mick's grin made her eyes sparkle.

"So am I." Hannah reclaimed her hand and picked up the menu. "Have you eaten here before?" She smiled at Mick.

"Once, when I first arrived. Isn't the cemetery near here?"

"Yes. It's two blocks down that way"—she pointed to the left—"just as you leave town."

"Yeah, then I've been here before. It's all a blur though. What do you recommend?"

"They make a really good taco salad, and the extreme burrito is my friend's favorite." Hannah shook her head at the unbidden thought of Charlie's favorite.

"What can I getcha?" The young, blonde waitress smiled at Hannah. "I already know what you want, hon." She looked at Mick. "What about you?"

"I think I'll give the taco salad a try."

"Good choice. Hannah here always has sweet tea. What would you like to drink?"

"The same." Mick smiled as the waitress walked away. "You must come here a lot."

"Not recently. I went to school with Haley. She always remembers what I like. In fact, when I come in here with my folks, she always knows what they like too."

"Thanks for giving me another chance, Hannah. I don't know what got into me. I'm really sorry for what I said."

"Thank you."

"I'm looking forward to getting to know you better."

"Me too." Hannah nodded. "Have you had any more ideas about renovating the house?"

"I've already bought the interior paint, and I've been asking around about hiring someone to do the outside and the roof."

"When you live on a farm all your life, like I have, you learn how to do almost everything. I can do the exterior painting, and I've replaced a roof or two in my life."

"I couldn't ask you to do that, Hannah. I can't pay you until the house sells."

Hannah's back stiffened when Mick mentioned selling the house.

"If I decide to stay there, then I don't know when I'd have enough money."

"I didn't ask to be paid, and as for helping you…. You didn't ask. I volunteered."

Their meals arrived and they tucked into them. Hannah noticed that every time she snuck a peek at Mick, she was doing the same thing. Inwardly, she smiled. It felt good to let someone else in.

Hannah put down her fork and leaned back. "I am stuffed."

"Me too." Mick smiled. "The food is delicious. I'm going to have to come back here."

"Yes, it is. I've never had a bad meal here." Hannah cocked her head to the right. "Did you know your grandpa owned an antique shop?"

"I knew he owned a store but never knew more than that. He never let me go with him to the store. He wanted me to stay home and study." Mick's eyes drifted to the table.

"You know, I think he saved all the good stuff when he quit the business. I bet it's all in that garage."

"Huh." Mick pursed her lips. "You might be right. It sounds like him. If you'd like to do it with me, we can check that out." Mick closed her eyes partially, before looking at the floor again. "If you want," she said softly.

"I'd love to help you, Mick. Who knows how much money you can make off the stuff. When do you want to start?"

"As much as I hate to say this, I need to get back to work right now. I'll be off for the next two days."

"I'll see you then." Hannah pushed back from the table. "Can I walk you back to the store?"

"I'd like that."

Hannah kept as close to Mick as she could and resisted the desire to hold her hand. She wanted to prolong their time together, as Wilkerson's came closer. "Sure you can't take the afternoon off?" she asked. "We could get started on going through the antiques."

"There's nothing I'd rather do, but I need to keep my job so I can pay the bills."

"I know." Hanna grinned. "I was hoping I could change your mind." They began walking again. Hannah reached out and took Mick's hand. "Is this okay?"

"Absolutely." The big smile on Mick's face confirmed the response.

Hannah gently squeezed the hand she was holding and let go when they reached the dry goods store. "When do you want to start on the garage?"

"How about tomorrow?" Mick motioned to the store. "I'd better get back to it. I'll see you tomorrow."

"Perfect." Hannah watched Mick walk into the store and could feel bubbles of happiness fill her. *Why did I spend all the years since high school grieving over Charlie?* Through the massive front window, she could see Mick talking with a man who was holding some sort of tool. Hannah grinned. *Life is good.*

†

Hannah walked into the kitchen and found her parents sitting at the table.

"Where've you been, girly? Sam asked. "We've gotta do maintenance on the tractors tomorrow. We ran them real hard plowin'."

"I'm afraid I can't help you, Daddy. I have plans for tomorrow and the next day." Hannah swallowed hard. She rarely ever told her daddy no.

"You will have to cancel those plans, girly, I need you here helpin' me."

"I can't." Hannah could see the anger rising on his face and shrugged. "Sorry."

"What's so important that you can't help me like you always do?"

"I've already made plans to help my friend Mick with her house tomorrow. I told you that last night, you told me we were goin' to take some time off."

"Who the hell is Mick?" Sam asked with a slight growl.

"What's wrong with your memory? I've already told you, Daddy, she's my friend."

"Well if she's a friend, then she will understand that you need to be here not there."

"Sam—"

"Keep out of this, Ada. It is between Hannah and me."

Hannah stood, rested her hands on the table, and fixed her jaw. "I have been here helpin' you out, Daddy, every day of the last seven and a half years. In all that time, I've never had a day off, and it's time I did. I will not be here to help you with the tractor tune-up for the next two days. Why don't you call one of your sons, if it's so urgent that it has to be done tomorrow?" She saw her father rub his neck but spun around on the heel of her boot and left the kitchen. The sounds of her parent's voices followed her.

"What was that all about? Is it her time of the month? She's never spoken to me like that."

"She's right, you know," Ada said.

"About what? I need her help."

"She's never taken a day to herself, Sam. Give her some days off and call Ryan Wills to come help, if fixing the tractors right now is so important. You did tell her she could take some time off."

Her mom's voice was the last thing Hannah heard before closing her bedroom door.

CHAPTER TWELVE

With tentative steps, Hannah entered the kitchen. She'd hoped her father had already eaten his breakfast and gone outside.

"Good morning," she said softly, as she moved to the refrigerator for the orange juice.

"Mornin'." Sam didn't look up from the paper he was reading.

Hannah held her breath, as she set her glass of juice on the table.

"Good morning," Ada said happily. "I saved a plate for you. I'll zap it for a minute."

"Thanks, Mama." Hannah peeked at her father. "Look, I'm sorry for what I said last night. If you can tell me the last day I had off—"

Sam finally looked up from his reading. "Yesterday. You had yesterday off. Besides it has nothin' to do with days off, Hannah. It has to do with your responsibility to this farm and your family."

Hannah swallowed hard. When he called her by her name and not girly, she knew he was pissed off. She pushed her chair back and stood. "Responsibility? Seriously, you are going to say that. I've dedicated everything to this place. I work here when I am sick, when it's freezing cold, when the wind is blowing so hard it's impossible to stand; I'm out there doing my job. I want to take a few days to do something other than farm work, and you throw a fit telling me I am neglecting the farm. Well, I'm not. I just want a few days to do something that I"—she pointed to her chest— "want to do."

"Then I guess you'd better go." Sam turned back to his paper. "I'll manage."

Hannah was conflicted. Her family was everything to her. She didn't want to hurt or disappoint her father. Yet, for the first time in years, she needed to hook up with someone other than family. She wanted to see what might develop with Mick.

"Now you two stop," Ada said. "Hannah, how many days do you need?"

"Two for now."

"Sam, can you do the tractor maintenance by yourself? I know you did it by yourself in the past."

"Sure. I can do it myself, but that isn't the point."

"What is the point?" Ada asked.

"Time spent with my daughter."

Hannah closed her eyes to hold back the tears.

"You get time with her every day, Sam, and you know it. She's going to go to town to help her friend out, like she promised. She will be here on Thursday to help you with the tractor." Ada looked at her daughter. "You go along. Will you be here for supper?"

"Not sure, Mama, probably not." Hannah kissed her mom's cheek. "Thank you." She leaned toward her daddy and kissed his cheek. "It's only two days, not a lifetime," she whispered before walking away.

†

Hannah sat in her truck in front of Mick's house for a minute. The feelings that were crying to be recognized felt right. She acknowledged her thoughts with a nod, before opening the truck door. Mick stood in the doorway with a crooked smile.

"You came."

"I told you I would. I always try to keep my word." Unable to stop herself, Hannah pulled Mick to her for a hug. They stayed that way for a minute, before Mick disengaged and smiled.

"Come on in. Have you had breakfast?"

Hannah thought of the meal that she didn't eat. "No, I haven't."

"Great. I made enough for two. Breakfast tacos okay with you?"

"One of my favorites."

"These are very good," Hannah said.

"Thanks. I've been thinking that we need to make a list of what needs to be done and prioritize."

"What do you think is the most important?" Hannah asked.

Mick laid a piece of paper on the table. "I've mapped this out. As you can see, I put the antiques at the top."

"Why is that?" Hannah asked, knitting her eyebrows.

"Well, since you thought there may be money in that stuff, we should take care of that first. It may turn out that there will be enough to hire someone to do all the big work."

"That sounds reasonable. Do you have a plan on how to do that?"

"First, I think we should take an inventory of everything. That includes taking pictures, along with brief descriptions. I figured that once we take an inventory, we can go to the antique shop I found online." She pointed her pencil at a name on the paper. "Ted's Antiquities and More. We can see if they'll give us a ballpark figure of what it's all worth. We can even take some of the smaller pieces with us."

"Seems like a good plan to me," Hannah said. "You're in luck; I happen to know Ted."

"Really? That is a plus."

She gave Mick a curious look. "It also sounds like you've done this before."

"No." Mick shook her head. "To experience organizing something to sell, you'd have to have something. I've never had anything in my life."

"Material things aren't important, Mick. If you have your integrity and power of self, you have it all. I know you do, because the easy thing would have been to stay where you were. You found a way to get here, and that comes from strength of character."

Mick looked away. "You give me too much credit. What do you say we head out to the garage and get started?"

Mick turned on the lights for the garage and waved a hand around the jam-packed room. "I looked in here yesterday and realized there wasn't enough light," Mick said. "I bought these really bright lights, so we can see what we have rather than dragging everything outside. If we need to have a closer look at anything, we can always take individual pieces outside."

"Good thinking." Hannah let her eyes survey the garage. "It looks like your grandpa arranged similar things together. This inventory might not take as long as we thought."

"Yeah, that's what I thought after I put the lights in." Mick slid her arm around Hannah's shoulders and squeezed her lightly. "Let's get started."

As they suspected, everything in the garage was arranged according to type. It didn't take long to make a list with photos of all the items. They loaded a few of the antiques in the bed of Hannah's truck and headed out. Ted's Antiquities was twenty miles away.

"How do you know the owner of Ted's?"

"Small town. Small school. Ted was several grades ahead of me. The antique store was his dad's. Ted Jr. took over the day to day running of the store a few years ago. I imagine he will have known your grandpa. His dad will certainly know of him."

"If he knew grandpa, then he will know the quality of the antiques he had, which will give us a good idea of their value."

Hannah reached over and took Mick's hand. "Even if you make enough money to fix up the house, I'd still like to do the exterior painting and roofing for you. That will probably cost the most. No sense spending all the money that you might get."

Mick entwined her fingers with Hannah's and smiled. "Thank you for everything. I'm so glad we met and are going on this adventure together."

You've given me life again. Hannah's heart soared at the thought. She glanced at Mick and smiled.

"Is that the store up there on the left?" Mick asked.

"Yep. We are now on the quest for antiquities." Hannah flicked on the blinker. Once the oncoming traffic cleared, she turned into the shop's parking lot.

"You'll do the talking right? I don't know this guy or anything about antiques."

"No worries, I've got your back."

"Hannah, it is so good to see you. I had no idea it was you that wanted my appraisal," Ted Martin said.

"Ted, this is my friend, Mick Hendricks. She's Tom Hendricks' granddaughter."

"I remember him. He only carried high-end antiques." Tom looked at Mick. "My condolences for your grandfather's passing."

"Thank you." Mick's gaze seemed to ask Hannah to take over the conversation.

"Ted, Mr. Hendricks left his house and a sizable antique collection to Mick. We have pictures of everything and brought some of the items with us. Do you think you can give us a ballpark price of the lot?"

Ted scratched his head. "Well, I guess I have time now to take a look at what you have." He looked at his wristwatch. "I can give you an hour or so."

"Fair enough," Mick said. "Shall we start with what we brought, then show you the pictures?"

"Yep, let's bring everything inside."

An hour and a half later, Ted looked up from the notebook he'd been writing in. He looked pleased with his work. "Your grandfather left you a sizable treasure, Ms. Hendricks."

"Really? That's fantastic." Mick grinned at Hannah.

"Ted, can you give us a value?"

"Oh no, I don't think I can. I will have to look at the pieces I haven't seen yet, then I need to research the values."

"Come on, Ted, you can give us an estimate can't you? Will she get enough to put a new roof on her house?"

"Probably."

"Oh." Mick looked away.

"Look, unseen, I can give you a ballpark of around seventy-five thousand, but you can't hold me to that number until I see it all."

"Fair enough." Mick held out her hand. "Thank you for your time. Let me know when you'd like to come by the house and look at everything."

"I'll check my calendar and get back to you in a day or two."

Hannah stepped forward and gave Ted a hug. "Thank you."

Mick and Hannah walked toward the truck and got in without a word, then grinned at each other.

"I can't believe it." Mick shook her head. "If the number he gave us is right, I must have a fortune sitting in that garage. And to think that it's been sitting in an unlocked garage for all this time."

"Things are looking up for you, Mick. What will you do with all that money?"

"I really haven't thought about it." Her phone rang. "I need to take this."

94

"Okay." Hannah didn't mean to listen to the one-sided conversation, but she had no choice.

"It worked out perfectly…Okay, we're on the road right now. I'll give you a call later tonight…Yeah, me too. Bye."

It was a curious sounding conversation. Hannah chastised herself for listening to the private communication. *I really didn't have a choice.*

"Sorry about that," Mick said. "It was a friend of mine checking up on me."

Hannah nodded. "Where did you grow up?"

"In Waco. I lived there until I was fifteen. After the divorce and my dad was gone for three years, my mom got remarried. The shit tried to molest me. I was eleven and my mom didn't believe me. She said I was jealous of her relationship with him and made up the story. That hurt me more than the molestation. So, I left and came here. I lived with my grandpa for five years before I moved on."

"Why didn't you live with your dad?"

"He died."

"Oh, I'm so sorry." Hannah gave Mick's hand a squeeze. "I don't remember ever seeing you at Three Junctions."

"My grandpa homeschooled me. Looking back on it, I probably should have gone to a proper school. I never really made any friends here. I kept to myself mostly. I was a tall gangly girl with stringy hair, and I didn't think anybody noticed me."

"How old are you?"

"I'm thirty-one."

"I pegged you for maybe twenty-eight."

Mick smiled. "Thanks for the compliment. How old are you?"

"I'll turn twenty-five in a few months."

"Hey, are you hungry? That Dairy Queen sign made my stomach growl."

"Sounds good to me. DQ it is. I think I might get a mint Oreo Blizzard." Hannah grinned. "Ice cream is good any time. I think it's a major food group."

Mick laughed. "I agree."

Back at Mick's house, they unloaded the truck and put it all back in the garage.

"Now that we know the value of all this stuff, I think I need to rebuild the garage and give it a new roof before working on the house." Mick held the kitchen door for Hannah to follow behind her. "I don't want to lose any of it."

"Hmm. It's been in there for a long time, so I don't think there's a rush to fix up the garage. A place to live is more important. The house might be where you need to start."

"Yeah I guess you're right." Mick winked. "Do you want something to drink?"

"No," Hannah whispered.

Mick stepped closer, put her arm around Hannah's shoulders, and ran a finger down her cheek. "I'd like to hold you in my arms." Mick bowed her head and kissed her.

The lips on hers were incredibly soft, and Hannah leaned into them. She was suddenly fifteen again, in the front seat of the very same truck she had been driving Mick around in. She pulled back and looked at Mick, refusing to let that memory linger. *That was then. This is now.* It was time to move forward, so she kissed Mick again with a fervor that she didn't know she still had.

When they broke apart, Mick was breathless. "I promise you will set the pace and choose how far you want to go."

Hannah swallowed hard. As much as she wanted more to happen, it was too fast for her. She stood straighter and took a step back. "I really need to get home. My folks will be waiting for me."

"Are you sure you aren't twelve years old and have to call Mommy and Daddy to tell them where you are and when you'll be home? Do you have a curfew, Hannah?" Mick spat out. "I really like you, Hannah. I don't like it when someone plays with me. I was hoping that we would— Never mind. Just go."

"Wait." Hannah grabbed Mick's hand. "I really like you too. It's just too soon for me. Please don't be angry with me. I'll be here in the morning and spend the day painting the interior." She watched Mick's jaw working back and forth.

"Do whatever you want." Mick shook her head. "I knew you wanted to take it slow, but when you set me on fire. I can't help being frustrated." She kissed Hannah softly then opened the door for her. "See you bright and early."

Hannah sat in her truck for a few minutes, debating whether to throw caution to the wind and just stay with Mick for the night. No, if she was going to do this, it would be slow and easy. She'd get to know Mick better, particularly since she seemed to have an erratic, hair-trigger temper. *I wonder if there's a red head in her family tree somewhere.* Nevertheless, there was no way she'd let herself be taken in again.

CHAPTER THIRTEEN

Music blared out the open truck windows on Hannah's early morning drive to town. She couldn't wait to see Mick. It had been a long time since feelings of happiness consumed her so much that it was impossible to stop smiling. When she stopped in Mick's driveway, her smile grew wider at the prospect of seeing her. She hopped out of the truck and walked with purpose to the front door, hoping that she wasn't too early. Although, a sleep-tousled Mick had its own appeal.

Mick was standing at the door dressed and ready for painting. Hannah was disappointed that she was dressed and tried not to sigh or pout.

"Hey, I was hoping you'd get here soon." Mick pushed open the screen door.

"Then I'm not too early."

"Nope, you're right on time." Mick winked at her. "Are you ready to paint?"

"Oh, I'm ready." Hannah grinned then pulled Mick to her. "Good morning," she said, before pressing her lips to Mick's.

Mick leaned into the kiss before taking a step back. "I like the way you greet the morning," she said with a grin. "The faster we paint, the sooner we can take a break and I can kiss you again."

"I like the sound of that." Hannah looked around the front room and saw that Mick had laid drop cloths over the furniture and along the exposed flooring. She took a coverall out of her bag and pulled it on over her clothes. "Well then, let's get to work."

The small room didn't take long to paint, and they moved on to the bedrooms.

"Thank goodness the rooms are small." Hannah was washing out her paint roller and Mick was leaning against the doorframe. "It's two thirty, why don't we take a break and have some lunch? I bought some lunchmeat and the fixin's, if you'd like that. If not, we can go somewhere" Mick said.

"I like sandwiches, and I'd rather have you to myself than in a crowded restaurant." Hannah could feel her face burn. It wasn't like her to make such a bold statement, not since high school anyway.

"Sounds perfect to me," Mick purred, as she pulled Hannah close and kissed her.

Hannah looked up at Mick. "It's been so long since I've felt like this. You are amazing." She leaned in for a kiss and ran her tongue over Mick's pliable lips. The tango began.

Mick kept kissing her while walking them to the couch. Soon, Hannah found Mick grinding on top of her. Her body was on fire with a need she'd long forgotten. She wanted it. Needed it. *Not like this. Not without love.* Not on scratchy old couch in a cluttered front room. She knew that she didn't know Mick well enough to love her yet. Hannah put her right hand on Mick's chest and pushed her away.

"What?" Mick looked confused.

Her spoken words echoed her thoughts. "I can't. Not like this. It's too soon. Mick, I'm sorry."

Mick nodded. "Sure, no hurry."

It was clear to Hannah that Mick was holding back the anger she'd displayed the night before. "Please understand, Mick," she pleaded. "I want to get this right between us and not end up as nothing other than a—"

"Quick fuck," Mick ground out. "You could have fooled me. You've been coming on to me ever since you got here."

"I'm sorry, that's not what I want." Hannah placed her palm on Mick's cheek and was glad that it wasn't swatted away. "My last relationship ended badly," she whispered. "I don't want to make that mistake again. I need to take it slow. Can you understand that?"

Mick blew out a breath. "It sounds to me as though you've already decided how this"—she moved a finger between them—"will go. I'm not out to take advantage of you or get you in bed and then dump you. I too want to see where this will take us."

"Please be patient with me," Hannah implored.

Mick pulled her close and kissed her forehead. "Of course, I will."

Hannah thought she could still see irritation simmering below the surface of Mick's actions and words. "I guess we'd better get back to painting. We don't have much left to do."

"Sure, I can do that after I make the sandwiches. Don't know about you, but I'm hungry."

Hannah watched Mick fix lunch and tried to understand her own mixed emotions. She couldn't deny her attraction to Mick, yet something was holding her back. Mick's angry outbursts were troubling. Perhaps she'd had a heartbreak too. Hannah fought the urge to go up to Mick and pull her close. It would only send the wrong message.

"Sandwiches are ready." Mick placed two paper plates on the worn kitchen table. "What do you want to drink?"

"Water is good."

They ate in silence and went back to painting the interior of the house.

†

Hannah drove back to the farm with thoughts of how her body reacted to Mick's touch. They hadn't talked much in the afternoon. The pat on her shoulder when Mick thanked her told a story in itself. Hannah had no doubt that she wanted to take the relationship further, but her inner voice was telling her to slow down. After all, she'd only known Mick for a few weeks. "I've got to decide what I want with Mick. Right now, all I'm doing is leading her on and shooting her down," she said to the empty truck. "I have to know in my heart that it's right." She pulled up to the house, turned off the engine, and got out.

"I'm home," Hannah called into the front room.

"I saved some supper for you," Ada said, as she came out of the kitchen. "Did you have a successful day?"

"Yeah, we painted all of the interior. When I get some time off again, I'll go help her with a new roof and painting the outside."

"What ever happened with the antiques in the garage?"

"We talked with Ted Martin. I think he will be out on Friday to look at everything." Hannah took a bite of steak. "I think Mick will make a lot of money on them."

"How are Ted and his dad doing?"

"Good, from what I could tell."

"Well, this Mick is lucky to have a friend like you to help." Ada sat down next to her. "I'm proud of you sweetheart." She leaned over and kissed her cheek.

"Mama, I'm so confused."

"About what?" Her mother had a puzzled look.

"Two things. Daddy and Mick. Why is Daddy being so grouchy lately? Nothing I do or say seems to make him happy."

"I think your Daddy is not feeling too good, but he's too stubborn to get help."

"Well, he needs to do something. I miss who he was."

"Me too. Now what about Mick?"

"I don't know what to do about her. I really like her, but my mind and heart are conflicted." Hannah put her fork down and closed her eyes.

"Tell me about what your feelings are."

"I want to take the relationship to the next level, but every time I think I'm ready to go there, I pull away."

"Why do you think you pull away?" Ada took her daughter's hand and held it.

"A little voice keeps telling me to stop. I think it scares me to make a commitment, Mama. What if it turns out like—"

"Charlie?"

"Yes."

"What if it doesn't? What if you find out that you care deeply for Mick?"

"I don't know, Mama, something tells me to…. Oh, I don't know what my problem is."

Ada pulled Hannah close. "Sweetheart, you have been happier than I've seen you in a very long time. Why not welcome back that happy girl you once were and stop living in the past? Give yourself and Mick a chance, and see where it goes. If you don't let anybody in, you will be alone all your life."

Hannah smiled and hugged her mom. "As always, you are the voice I needed to hear. Thank you for being here for me."

"Any time, sweetie."

CHAPTER☐OURTEEN

It was cotton-planting time. Hannah and her father were working dusk to dawn. The only time Hannah had to speak with Mick was in the evening. Their conversations were usually brief, since she found it hard to keep her eyes open. Finally, the planting was finished, and she was on her way to Mick's house to start on the roof. When the house came into view a huge smile covered Hannah's face. She saw Mick on a ladder, painting the house. She tooted the horn and waved.

"Hey, beautiful, would you like some help?" Hannah called out.

Mick climbed down the ladder and greeted Hannah with a hug. "It's great to finally see you again. I've missed you." She turned to the house. "What do you think?"

"It looks great. Is this all you have left?"

"Yep. That and the roof."

"What about the garage?"

"I'm still waiting for Ted to come and make an offer."

"Really? He seemed so enthusiastic when he came here."

"Yeah, that's what I thought, but I've heard nothing since." Mick shrugged.

Hannah shook her head. "That's weird. I definitely got the vibe that he was very interested in buying the lot. Why don't I give him a call and see what's up?"

"I can't ask you to do that, Hannah."

"You didn't ask, I volunteered." Hannah took out her phone and dialed the number. "I'll put it on speaker."

"Ted's Antiquities how may I help you?"

"Ted?"

"Yes."

"This is Hannah Garvin."

"Hannah, I don't see or hear from you in years, and here you're calling me twice in a month. What can I do for you?"

"I'm here with my friend, Mick, with my phone on speaker. We were wondering about what you thought of her grandpa's antiques. It's been a while since you came out to look at them."

"Ah, yes. A very interesting collection. I'm waiting for my business partner to get back from Dallas. He's speaking with dealers there, and I'd like his input. Your friend has a high-end collection. Frankly, I doubt we can sell the valuable items in our store. We just don't get that type of traffic. Oh, we can sell the old phones and items like that but not the paintings or that cherry writing desk that I think is from the 1850s. There are dealers in bigger markets like Dallas or Houston that will be very interested."

"So you'd act as a go-between," Mick said.

"Yes."

"And your commission would be?" Mick asked.

"I think twenty percent would be fair," Ted said in a tentative voice.

"I think ten percent is fair, Ted. I can't see that a trip to Dallas would be worth more."

"We have the connections, Mick, and those are invaluable."

"All I need to do is search for the phone numbers on the internet make the calls myself. Ten percent is the maximum I'd pay."

Hannah listened to the conversation, feeling a bit squeamish. She stopped the speaker and put the phone to her ear. "Ted, let me know when your partner gets back, and we'll hammer out the details." She listened. "Okay, talk to you then."

"Why'd you do that?" Mick demanded. "I was negotiating with him."

Hannah chewed on her lip, trying to get her emotions under control. "Because now is not the time for that discussion. Ted is doing you a favor by finding a buyer for the antiques. He could have told you there was nothing of value, but he didn't. In fact, a few weeks ago, you were ready to haul everything to the dump. Now you're trying to negotiate a commission for them. Ted could easily have made a low bid, then taken the lot to Dallas and made more money for himself. He hasn't. He is trying to be fair," Hannah said with emphasis.

Mick looked down and kicked the dirt. "You're right," she mumbled. "He is your friend and is probably trying to do a favor for you. What a shit I am. Will you call him back so I can apologize?"

"No. He'll call when he knows something." Hannah caressed Mick's sad looking face. "Come on, let's get the painting finished, then we can start on the roof."

It was nearly supper time when they finished the exterior painting, including the garage. "Looks good doesn't it?" Mick asked.

"Yes it does. Why don't we get cleaned up and go to my house for dinner? Mama said you were welcome to join us."

"Really?" Mick's eyes opened wide. "Are you sure?"

"Yes, now let's wash up and go. Daddy likes his supper at exactly six."

†

"Thank you, Mrs. Garvin, for inviting me to dinner," Mick said.

"Glad you could join us. Your grandfather was a very special man. We miss him every Sunday at church. No one sang a song with as much gusto as he did."

"I remember, when I was living with him, that he would sing all the time." Mick smiled sadly. "I miss him very much."

"Is supper ready?" Sam stopped short when he saw Mick. "Who are you?"

Hannah cringed at her father's brusque tone.

"Hi, I'm Mick Hendricks." Mick held out her hand.

"Right, you're that new friend of my daughter. You've got her helpin' you to fix up your grandpa's house for nothin'. Right?"

Hannah saw Mick ball a fist. "Daddy, I offered."

"Yes, sir. She's been a great help and really knows all about repairs."

"I taught her all she knows." Sam puffed out his chest, then looked at Ada. "So is supper ready?"

"Let's all sit." Ada gestured toward the kitchen. "We have pot roast and roasted carrots and potatoes."

Once they were all seated, Hannah took Mick's hand and her father's on the other side of her. Before Hannah bowed her head, she noticed the look of disinterest on Mick's face.

"Father, please nourish not only our body but our soul," Ada prayed.

Hannah and her parents said, "Amen," in unison, while Mick remained silent. She didn't reciprocate when Hannah squeezed her hand before letting go. They all ate in companionable silence until Hannah said, "Mick's house is almost done."

"Good, then you can get back here and help me. I'm tired of doin' your work too." Sam looked at Mick. "What kinda name is Mick for a girl?"

"Daddy!" Hannah scolded.

"My given name is Michelle. When I was born, my older brother called me Mick and it stuck."

"Are your folks from around here?" Ada asked

"No, I grew up in Colorado."

Hannah shook her head wondering if she'd heard right. She opened her mouth to ask Mick a question but was interrupted.

"Are you gonna sell that house and move back home?" Sam asked.

"Not sure, sir. I've grown used to the town, and I like the people around these parts." Mick smiled at Hannah, before she scooted her chair back some. "I need to get going soon. Thank you for the wonderful dinner, Mrs. Garvin. It's been a long time since I've had anything so delicious."

"You're welcome, Mick. Come join us for supper any time you can."

"You may be sorry you said that." Mick laughed. "I do love to eat."

Sam scraped his chair across the floor and stood. "Time for the news. I hope they say we're gonna get some moisture. You comin'?" He headed for the front room.

"I'll be there as soon as I'm done with the dishes." Ada stood and began clearing the table.

"Mama, we can do that. Go ahead and watch your show."

Ada smiled. "I can't let company do the dishes. Besides, I thought you needed to go, Mick."

"I have enough time to do the dishes, Mrs. Garvin. I'm not a stranger to hot soapy water and a sink full of dishes."

"Are you sure?"

Mick nodded.

"Well, okay then." Ada left the kitchen.

"You wanna wash or dry?" Hannah asked.

Mick looked toward the front room. "I'd rather do this." She leaned over and kissed Hannah.

Hannah pulled away. "Not here and not now. When I walk you out to your grandpa's old truck—"

"I'll get lucky?"

"Something like that."

After they'd stepped away from the front porch, Hannah said, "I noticed you didn't bow your head when Mama said the prayer at supper."

"I'm not religious. Never have been. When I lived here, Grandpa tried to get me to go to church with him, but I always refused."

"Why? I'm not judging. I just wonder why you don't believe."

"Because," Mick blew out a breath. "If there was a God who looked over us, there wouldn't be so much hatred and anger in the world."

"There's a reason for everything, Mick. We just have to realize it when it happens."

"Okay. Do you mind if we don't have this conversation? I really need to get back to town. I'm expecting a phone call."

"Sure."

When they got to the truck, Mick took Hannah in her arms and pulled her close. "Are you ready to get lucky?" she asked.

"Well, that is what you promised." Hannah let Mick pull her into a kiss. She kissed her back, not letting her lips linger for more than a second.

"Is something wrong?" Mick asked.

"No," Hannah lied. She felt uncomfortable standing in front of her home kissing Mick. "I'm just tired. We did a lot of work today."

"Yes, we did. When will I see you again?"

"In a few days. There's work I need to do here."

"Okay. Give me a call when you're on your way." Mick leaned in, and Hannah turned her head. Mick frowned. "What?"

"Mama, is looking out the front window."

"We certainly don't want to frighten her by knowing her daughter likes to kiss," Mick said sarcastically. She opened the truck door and got in. "See you later."

Hannah watched Mick drive away and tried to make sense of her unchecked emotions. Would Mick's belief that there was no God be a deal breaker? *Is it that big of a deal?* "Time will tell, I guess." When she couldn't see Mick's truck's lights any longer, she turned and went into the house.

CHAPTER □ I□ TEEN

Hannah stood across the street from Mick's house and took a picture with her camera. She framed it carefully, so that Mick was in the picture standing on the front porch. "Perfect," she said after she ran across the street.

"I still can't believe we got this done so fast," Mick said. "Someone stopped by this morning and wanted to know who I used to restore the house." She laughed. "I told him Hendricks and Garvin then advised him that they had retired."

"Hey, if you want to get away from Wilkerson's you can always go into home repairs."

"Naw, I'm not good enough to do that."

"Sure you are, Mick. I've seen your work. It's fantastic."

"We'll see. You want to come inside? I cleaned and even changed the sheets." Mick wiggled her eyebrows. "If you're interested that is."

"As tempting as that is, I'm afraid I need to get back to the farm. My daddy isn't feeling well. It's up to me to pull the knifing sled on the fields."

"Knifing? What's that?"

"It is a way of getting rid of the weeds between the plants. A tractor pulls the sled."

"How long will it take? Maybe you can come back tonight." She shrugged. "I guess you won't be on the tractor then."

"Sounds like a plan. Why don't I give you a call before I leave?" She looked directly into Mick's brown eyes. "I want to let go of the past, Mick, and I'm ready to do that with you."

"Perfect." Mick moved closer and pulled Hannah into a hug. "I want you," she whispered. "Hurry back. I'll be ready for you."

†

Ada was waving frantically, as Hannah pulled the truck into the yard. She jumped out and ran to the porch. "What's wrong?" she asked.

"It's your daddy. I don't know what's wrong with him. He said he can't catch his breath. He's sweating so much, I keep having to change his shirt."

Hannah raced into the house and saw her father flat out on the couch and breathing heavily. She fell to her knees and touched his forehead. He was burning up. "Mama, call for an ambulance." She felt for his pulse. It seemed rapid to her.

Hannah stood to grab a blanket from the back of the couch. As she laid it over him, she noticed just how thin he'd gotten.

"The ambulance is on the way. They said to wipe him with cold cloths to help keep the fever down."

"When did this start?"

"Oh, I don't know. He was out fixing the tractor, then came in saying he didn't feel well. The next thing I knew, he was lying on the floor."

"Was he clutching his chest?"

"No, he just said he couldn't catch his breath."

In the distance, Hannah could hear the wail of the siren and let out the breath she'd been holding.

"The ambulance is here," Ada cried.

"Come on in." Hannah ushering the paramedics into the front room. She quickly informed them of what her mother had said and let them do their work."

Hannah held her arm around her mother's shoulders and pulled her close. They anxiously watched the medics examine Sam.

When they began to load Sam on the stretcher, Ada asked, "Did he have a heart attack?"

"Can't say right now, ma'am. We need to wait to see what the doc says." The medics lifted the stretcher and rolled it out to the ambulance.

†

They had been sitting impatiently in the waiting room for half an hour. Hannah got up and went to the reception desk.

"Can you help me please?" She gave the woman at the desk a weak smile. "My father was brought in by ambulance, almost thirty minutes ago, and we have heard nothing."

"What's the name?" the older woman asked.

"Sam Garvin."

"Give me a minute, and I'll go check on him."

Hannah felt her phone vibrate and looked at the read out. *Damn.* "Hi, Mick. I'm sorry I haven't called you. I'm at the hospital.... My dad had a heart attack, I think.... That's not necessary...Oh, okay, I'd appreciate that."

The nurse returned. "Ms. Garvin, the doctor is with your father right now. She is waiting for some results, then she'll be out to speak with you and your mother."

"Thank you." Hannah walked over to her mother. "They're waitin' on test results."

"He has to be okay. What will I do without him?" Her mother's tear-filled eyes looked up at her.

"No talkin' like that, Mama. He is strong. Whatever it is, the doctors will fix him."

"I need to call the boys."

"Let's wait till we have something to tell them. Okay."

"You're right." Ada wiped at her eyes and blew her nose.

Ten minutes later, the outside door swung open and Mick walked hurriedly into the waiting room. Hannah stood and went to Mick, who engulfed her in her arms. "Thank you for coming." Hannah buried her face in Mick's shoulder, trying to compose herself. She needed to be strong for her mother, and that meant no tears.

"Shh, I'm here. You can lean on me."

Hannah pulled back. "Are you for real?" she said softly while trying to stop the tears. "Thank you, Mick. I'm so glad you came."

"Mrs. Garvin," a woman in a white lab coat called out.

"That's me." Ada rose from her chair.

"I'm Dr. Monroe. Your husband is resting. He was severely dehydrated, and we've treated that—"

"Then he didn't have a heart attack?" Ada blurted.

"There is no indication that he had one. However, we've done tests and are waiting for the results before we know more. He is stable, but just."

"Did this happen from his dehydration?"

"No," Dr. Monroe said. "There's more going on. That's why I ordered the other tests."

"What are the other tests for?" Hannah asked.

"We can discuss all that when we know what we are dealing with."

"Can I see him?" Ada asked.

"I'm sending him to ICU. You can see him when he's settled." Dr. Monroe squeezed Ada's arm.

"ICU!" Ada's eyes were wide. "I thought you said you treated him."

"We treated him for the dehydration, Mrs. Garvin. He's still very sick, and we need to monitor him closely."

"I want to know what's wrong with him now," Ada demanded.

"Mama, they don't know yet. When they get the test results back, they will let us know. It won't be long." Hannah looked at Dr. Monroe. "Right?"

"Mrs. Garvin, I am an ER doctor. Your husband needs a specialist. Please be patient and let us figure out what is going on with him. It shouldn't be much longer."

Hannah put her arm around her mother's shoulders. "How long before we can see him, Doctor?"

"Probably in a half hour, maybe less. If you go to the second floor waiting room, they will come get you when they have your father settled."

"Thank you." Hannah turned to her mother and Mick. "Come on, let's find the cafeteria and get a bite to eat. I'm starving."

"No," Ada said. "I'm going to the waiting room."

"Mama, when was the last time you ate?"

"I don't know. I just want him to be okay." Ada began crying again.

Hannah put her arm around her mother. "Come on, let's go to the other waiting room."

"I'll find the cafeteria and get us all something to drink at least," Mick said. "What would you like?"

"Tea is good." Hannah, fearful of what was to come, led her tearful mother to the elevators. She called over her shoulder. "Thanks, Mick… for everything."

†

A new doctor joined Dr. Monroe, who approached Ada, Hannah, and Mick in the family waiting room. "This is Dr. Murray. Would you come with us to a private room, where we can talk?" Dr. Monroe asked.

Ada and Hannah got up to follow the doctor, and Hannah looked around to see where Mick was. "Are you coming?"

Mick shook her head. "No, this is for you and your mom. I'll be here when you're done."

Hannah nodded and went into the room. Dr. Murray shut the door.

"We've gotten the test results back, Mrs. Garvin, and they confirm that your husband has Chronic Lymphocytic Leukemia."

Hannah kept a firm grip on her mother's hand. "What is the prognosis?"

117

"The cancer is advanced," Dr. Monroe said. "We don't have what he needs for treatment here. We need to transfer your father to a hospital that is better equipped to treat him for the cancer."

"We want the best for him. Where do you recommend?"

"The best place for your father is M.D. Anderson Cancer Center in Houston. It is ranked the best in the country and is his best hope. We can arrange to have him transferred there."

"That's so far away. I don't know if I can be away from him," Ada said.

"There are places for families to stay," the doctor offered.

"If going there will bring him back home without the disease, then that is where we will go." Ada wiped at the tears rolling down her cheeks. "Can I see him now?"

"Yes."

Still holding her mother's hand, Hannah followed the doctors into her father's ICU room. They stood next to the bed looking down at the man who'd been their rock for years. He appeared small and frail.

Ada took his hand and he opened his eyes. She smiled and leaned down to kiss his cheek. "We will get through this," she whispered.

"Yes, we will," Hannah said. "I'll go out so you two can talk." She made her way out of the ICU and back to Mick in the waiting room.

"How is he?" Mick asked

"He has leukemia." Hannah broke down. She was glad that Mick was there to comfort her, for she was feeling lost and alone.

†

Sam was transferred to M. D. Anderson Cancer center the next day, and the family converged there. After the hugs and hellos, Mack asked, "What do we do now?"

"Right now, they're running more tests for their own evaluation," Ada said.

"Why?" Bo asked. "They only do that so they can get more money," he growled. "Isn't having leukemia a good enough diagnosis?"

"Settle down," Ada said. "This is the best hospital for him, so we will trust that they are doing what is needed."

"Mama is right," Hannah said. "We need to find a place for Mama to live while she's here. They gave us a list of places to check out. We need to make sure she's in a place where she feels comfortable."

Time went by in a blur. They settled on a place for Ada to stay that was within walking distance from the hospital. Over the two days, they discussed treatments and the odds of remission with the oncologist.

They were gathered in Sam's room.

"Daddy we'll be back in a few weeks for a visit," Bo said.

"What I'd like you to do is go help your sister. It's a big job runnin' the place by herself, and it's time for you both to step up."

Hannah watched, as her brothers looked down at their feet.

"Daddy, don't worry about the farm. I've got it under control." She grinned. "After all, I had the best teacher."

"That you did." Sam yawned.

"We need to get to the airport," Hannah said. "After I drop the boys off, I'll come back to say good-bye. Like you always tell me, Daddy, we can't keep burnin' daylight."

"Before you go, I want you boys to promise to help your sister out."

"We will, Daddy," Bo and Mack said in unison.

After everything was settled, Hannah began the long, lonely trip back home.

†

Hannah was up before the sun and collapsed in her bed after dark. She did all of the farm work. Her brothers hadn't appeared to help like they promised.

"Sorry, Sis, the kids have the flu. I'm hoping that once things settle down, I'll be able to help you," Bo had said.

"Sis, I've got month end reports to get out. I can't come now, but I will as soon as I can," Mack told her.

It wasn't a surprise to Hannah that they had bailed on her, but it still hurt. Two weeks of going solo had left her ragged. Hannah stood in a dark house, preparing to face another day. She heard honking and looked out the window. The rising sun backlit a silhouette. Mick.

Hannah's heart soared.

"I came to help," Mick said, when Hannah opened the door.

Hannah pulled her in close and began to cry. "Thank you," she sobbed. "I'm sorry I haven't called you. By the time I finish for the day, I'm so exhausted, all I can manage is to go to bed."

Mick held her at arm's length. "Have you been eating?"

Hannah shook her head. "Not much. Cereal mostly." She shrugged. "Ran out of that last week, I think. I did buy some frozen foods and eat them when I remember."

120

"It's time to take a day off," Mick said. "You won't do your family any good if you run yourself into the ground. Where are your brothers? I thought they were going to help."

"They came out last weekend and helped for a day and a half, but then had to get back to their jobs and families." Hannah shook her head. "I hoped for more but wasn't surprised."

"We can figure out what to do so you have some help. First, let's see what you have in the refrigerator and I'll make you breakfast. After that, you can show me what I can do to help. I don't know much about farming, but I can learn."

"I'd appreciate that."

Mick opened the refrigerator door and shook her head with eyes wide. "How many eggs do you have in here?" She laughed and shook her head again. "You should set up a stand on the road and sell them."

"They've kinda got away from me. At first I'd make them for a meal, but then I wanted to sleep more than eat."

Mick shook her head. "Well, this morning, you are going to have a decent breakfast." She looked at the abundance of eggs in the refrigerator. "Why don't I take all these eggs with me and give them away at Wilkerson's?"

"Sounds good to me."

After a hearty breakfast, Hannah began to show Mick all that she accomplished in a typical day. It soon became evident that farm work was not something in Mick's wheelhouse.

"I had no idea how much you do," Mick said when they finished for the day.

"Yeah, it makes for a long day when you do it yourself." Hannah patted Mick's back. "Thanks for the help. Have you heard from Ted?"

"Yes, he came by last week to arrange for someone from an antique shop in Austin to come look at everything. He comes tomorrow."

"Did Ted give you any idea of how much is a fair price?"

"We discussed that, but his recommendation is to wait and see. He said they'd give me a low ball price at first and warned me not jump at that."

"Sounds like a good plan." Hannah hugged Mick close and kissed her cheek. "I've missed you. Things have been so crazy over the last weeks."

"How's your dad doing?"

"He's getting really strong chemo. My mother stays by his side between treatments. It sounds like they're rough on him. The doctors are cautiously optimistic." Hannah blew out a breath. "He's still really sick."

"Is there anything I can do to help you?"

Hannah shook her head. "I don't think so."

"Come on, let's get you something to eat, then put you in bed."

Hannah gratefully acquiesced. It had been too long since someone took care of her.

Lying in bed, with Mick's arm around her, felt safe. She fell into a dreamless and restorative sleep for the first time in weeks.

The next morning, Hannah woke and was disappointed that Mick wasn't there. Instead, she found a note.

H, I had to get home so I can get ready for the antique guy. I will call you later. M

Dressed and ready for the day, Hannah was about to leave the house when she heard knocking on the front door.

"Who can that be?" When she opened the door, the minister from the church was at the door with his wife. "Pastor and Mrs. Webster, this is a nice surprise."

"Hannah dear, we wanted to stop by and bring you a casserole and a pie. It can't be easy doing everything by yourself," Doris Webster said. "We saw the girl from Wilkerson's giving out eggs and asked her where she got so many. She told us from you."

"We had no idea you were here alone. The last we heard, your brothers were here helping out," Pastor Webster said.

"Thank you, please come in." Hannah opened the door wide and moved to let them by. "Please excuse the dust. I just haven't had the time to do housework too."

"How's your daddy doing?" Pastor Webster asked.

"It's early yet. He's doing heavy doses of chemo, and it's a wait and see kind of thing."

"Hannah, I've been talking to the parishioners. They're organizing it so that some of them can come here each week to help you." The pastor waved his hand. "By just looking at you, I can see that you're wearing yourself out. Please, let us help you."

Hannah leaned against the back of the couch, trying to get hold of her emotions. "Thank you," she whispered. "I am near my breaking point."

The pastor took her hand and held it. "Pray with me."

Hannah nodded and bowed her head.

"Lord, we wait upon you, knee deep in the water of life, expectant and hopeful. May the waves of the Holy Spirit be upon us, ministering to the pain, smoothing over wounds, and wrapping your faithful servant Sam with peace. Amen."

There was no stopping the tears. Not only was Hannah worn out with all the farm work, but her mind never stopped worrying about her daddy. She needed his steady strength and encouragement.

Doris pulled her close. "We are all praying for your daddy. We know he will overcome. You must always keep that certainty in your heart. God will not let you down."

"Thank you." Hannah looked at both of them. "You have lifted a great burden off my heart."

"We must go now," the pastor said. "Patrick Heffner will be in touch with you, Hannah, about arranging help."

"And I will be in charge of making sure you get at least one good meal a day. You are getting too skinny, but we will take care of that." Doris hugged her. "Keep the faith, my dear."

Once they left, Hannah called Mick to give her the good news and thank her for giving out the eggs. The call went to voice mail. "Mick, I just had a visit from Pastor Webster and his wife. They are arranging for neighbors to help on the farm. Thank you for taking care of me yesterday."

Charlie

CHAPTER ☐ IXTEEN

Pastor Webster and his wife were true to their words, allowing her to get the rest and nourishment she needed. Hannah felt a sense of well-being and hope.

"Good morning, Nelly. Right on time. Come on in. I just made coffee."

"That sounds good. You know, I never drank coffee until I started working at the school." Nelly laughed. "I remember when I drank some in front of your mama. I thought her jaw was gonna hit the floor."

"That's funny." Hannah grinned as she poured two cups of coffee. "Come on and sit with me, then I'll help you collect the eggs."

Nelly looked at her wristwatch. "Okay. I have time. Since we've been giving your eggs away at the church, there's been a line waiting for me."

"I'm glad you can use them like that." Hannah grinned and shook her head. "They were getting away from me. I almost ran out of refrigerator space."

"How are volunteers working out? Do they come when they should?"

"Yes. It's a big help. For all the help and meals, I'm grateful."

"Well, I gotta get going." There was a knock on the door." Why don't you get that? I'll gather the eggs and get on my way."

"Okay. Thanks, Nelly."

Hannah opened the front door and saw Bobby Gaines standing there. "Good morning, Mr. Gaines. Are you my helper for the day?"

"I sure am. How's your daddy doin'?"

"Still early days, Mr. Gaines. He's undergoing intensive chemo. Mama says it is hard on him."

"I imagine it would be. Your daddy wasn't one to admit he needed help or that he was feeling bad."

"Yeah, he's stubborn. That's for sure."

"Well, I'll get started."

"Okay. I'll get my gloves and be right out in a few minutes." For the next three hours, Hannah worked with Charlie's father. Never once did she ask about his daughter.

"I'll be back at the same time next week, Hannah."

"Thank you, Mr. Gaines, I appreciate all your help." She gestured toward the cotton field. "Six hundred forty acres is a lot of work."

"That it is. I can't believe you worked this all by yourself. Take care, Hannah. If you need anything, please don't hesitate to call."

"Will do." She watched the man walk to his truck and waved just before her phone rang. She pressed the speaker button. "Hey, Mick, do you want to come for supper tonight? I have a refrigerator full of food."

"Maybe, but right now I need you here. Ted and the guy from Austin are coming at three this afternoon. Can you come?"

Hannah looked around and saw about three jobs she needed to take care of immediately. "I can be there as long as I get things done here first." She shrugged. "I'll be there. You can count on me."

"Perfect. Guess what?"

"What?" Hannah was itching to get her work done so she'd be there on time.

"I don't know how we missed it, Hannah, but in a drawer of a small desk was a journal. Apparently, Grandpa had inventoried everything in the garage along with prices."

"Wow! That will give you a good frame of reference when the antique guy makes an offer."

"Exactly. I added everything together. The sum is quite a bit more than what Ted quoted."

"Well, don't count on that too much. We always think our stuff is worth more than it is."

"Yeah, I guess you're right. Do you think you'll be here before they come, so we can go over this?"

"I'll be there as soon as I can, Mick. No guarantees. There are jobs that need to be done before I can go."

"I thought you had people helping you out."

"I do. Today's helper has already been here and gone. There's a lot of work that needs doing on a farm, Mick. You saw only a small part of it the other day. Please understand that I can't just walk away whenever I want. I will be there as soon as I can. I'll give you a call when I leave."

"Okay." The dejection in Mick's voice was obvious.

†

Hannah had called ahead and arrived at Mick's house at two fifteen. She was greeted with coolness. *Yikes, maybe I should have kept working at home instead of coming here.* "Will you show me the journal?" she asked tentatively.

"That's why you came, isn't it? Here." Mick shoved the small, leather-bound journal in her direction.

"I came to see you too, Mick," Hannah whispered. She skimmed through the book, noting familiar items. She had a reasonably good idea of what they were worth back in the day, shopping with her grandmother. "I imagine the values in here reflect a selling price in his store."

"Yeah, I guess."

"Hey, what's the matter? If you don't want me here, say so and I'll go. I left stuff undone so I could be here for you."

"I'm sorry. Please stay. I suddenly realized, when I saw that book, just how much my life will be impacted if the values are even close." Mick chewed on her lip. "It will be life changing."

"Yes, it will." Hannah stood in the driveway. Ted and an older woman get out of a car and walked toward them. "Hi, Ted," she said.

"Good afternoon, ladies. This is Rachel Heath. Rachel, this is Mick Hendricks, who owns the collection, and her friend, Hannah Garvin."

"It's good to meet you, Rachel," Mick said.

128

Rachel shook hands with each of them. "Pleased to meet you both. I have seen the photos of your collection, Ms. Hendricks. If you will allow me, I'm eager to inspect everything."

"Please go in the garage and take a look," Mick said. "It's tight on space in there, but I think I've made paths to everything."

Hannah and Mick stood at the fringes of the garage, as Rachel examined each piece. Occasionally, she would say something to Ted that was indistinguishable to them. Finally, Rachel nodded and walked toward them.

"Ms. Hendricks, you have a remarkable collection here. I haven't seen many of these items in years. They are mostly in good condition, except some will need extensive restoration work." Rachel looked back over the garage and its contents. "Do you have an idea on how much you'd like for the entire collection?"

"My grandpa was an antiques dealer. I found an inventory of everything in here, along with the condition and his assessment of the values."

"That's good to know," Rachel said. "Have you added it all up?"

"I have, but you will have to keep in mind that this"—she held up the book—"is nine years old."

"And?"

"His estimate was eighty-five thousand dollars."

"How about fifty-five?" Rachel countered.

"I'm afraid you've wasted your time, Ms. Heath. The price I gave you was wholesale, not retail."

"I'm sure we can come to some kind of understanding, Ms. Hendricks." Rachel looked back at the garage. "Let me take another look."

An hour later, they were discussing a pickup date. Mick folded a check for seventy thousand dollars, before slipping it in her back pocket."

Hannah was sitting next to Mick on the couch in her front room. "Are you sure you haven't been in sales before? You handled her magnificently."

"It was the look on her face when she looked back at everything. It told me she'd deal. I could see she wanted it." Mick leaned in and kissed Hannah gently. "Just like I want you."

The kisses soon became passionate. Hannah, wanting to take the relationship to the next step, still pushed away.

"What's wrong *now*?" Mick was obviously perturbed.

"Mick, I want you, but right now I have too much going on to follow my heart. Can you understand that?"

"I can understand that you keep saying you want more but keep pushing me away. I don't like being treated like that, Hannah. I don't know how much longer I want to play this game with you."

"It's not a game, Mick. It won't be long, I promise. I want to give you the relationship you deserve. Can you understand that, right now, my brain is too jumbled? My brother Bo sent iPads to me and my parents, so we can Skype with them." Hannah looked at Mick. "I think, once I can see my dad, it will settle me down and I can concentrate on you."

"How are you going to Skype? I recall you telling me that Internet connections where you live are sketchy, at best."

"They are. I thought I would go to the café and use their Internet. Maudie won't mind."

"Why don't you come here?"

"Really?"

"Of course."

"Thank you, thank you." Hannah grinned and hugged Mick. "Who knows what will happen after I'm done talking with my family?"

"Good things I hope."

†

Satisfied with the day's work, Hannah collected her new iPad and got in her truck. She couldn't wait to get to Mick's house and connect with her parents. Her heart ached for them. It seemed that she hadn't seen them in a very long time, but it had only been a month.

She wasn't able to pull her pickup into Mick's driveway. Another car blocked the driveway, and Mick's old pickup wasn't anywhere to be seen. "Huh. Looks like she spent some of that money already."

Hannah hopped out of her truck and headed for the front door. She did her usual 1-2-3 knock and was surprised when a stranger opened the door."

"Can I help you?" a tall blonde asked.

"I'm looking for Mick. We were supposed to meet."

"Oh, you must be Hannah. Aren't you the woman that helped her renovate this house?"

"Yes, that's me. Is she here?"

"She's taking a shower at the moment. Come on in." The woman opened the screen door wide. "I'm Jamie Hendricks, Mick's wife."

Hannah looked past the woman and saw Mick, who was obviously just out of the shower. She came to the door and took the blonde's arm and pulled her away. "What the hell do you think you're doing, Jamie?" Mick growled. "Hannah, this isn't what you think."

"Oh, I'm sure it is." Hannah shook her head. "You must have seen me coming from a mile away. Some country bumpkin, farm girl you could manipulate and take advantage of," she spat out.

"No, it wasn't like that at all. Please, come in so I can explain," Mick implored.

"I don't think there is anything you can tell me that I'd believe. You neglected to tell me that you have a wife, Mick. Didn't you think that was something relevant?" Hannah clenched her teeth, grinding out her anger. "What a fool I am. I actually believed you cared."

"Hannah, please I do care. I promise it's not what Jamie made it out to be."

"Really? Does that mean you two aren't married?"

"No, we are. It's only for tax reasons."

Hannah laughed. "Yeah right, pull the other one. I thought you had to hitchhike here because you didn't have any money. Why the hell would you need to be married for *tax* reasons? Do you really think I'm that stupid?" She turned and walked away with Mick following her."

"Please don't go," Mick pleaded. "Let me explain."

Hannah spun around and slapped Mick's face. "There's nothing you can say to me that will ever let you into my life again." She hoisted herself into her truck and slammed the door. She gunned the engine and left Mick behind.

†

Stunned, Hannah sat in her truck, outside of Rosie's Cantina. "Can it be true? Does Mick have a wife?" She shook her head and put it out of her mind. She needed to speak with her parents, who always grounded her when she needed it the most. This was such a time. She saw that she could access the Internet to make a Skype connection and was glad something was going right. She pressed the send button, hoping it would work. It wasn't long before she heard the Skype melody.

"Daddy." She held her hand up to the screen and touched his face.

"It's me, girly, or what's left of me."

Hannah took in the frail man who had once seemed so invincible to her. Tears stabbed at her eyes. Yet, she needed to remain strong. Her father was having a hard enough time, without her showing her emotions. "I miss you so much. It's not the same without you workin' by my side."

"I'm sorry I left you with so much to do, girly."

"Don't worry about that. Your favorite forty-two players come by and help out all the time. They told me the dominoes miss you." The smile that her words brought to her father's face warmed her heart. "Besides the church women, the Masons and Mama's Eastern Star ladies come by also."

"That's not right," Sam said. "I should be there workin' and not them."

"You concentrate on getting better. When you come back home, I'll send them all on their way. You always helped out all our neighbors over the years, so let them pay you back. It's only right."

"Hi, sweetheart," Ada said. "Have you been eating right? You look like you've lost a lot of weight."

"Mama, I'm doin' fine now. There's a bunch of the church ladies bringin' food all the time. You won't believe all the meals I've had to freeze." Hannah laughed. "I finally had to tell them that it was only me they were feedin'."

"Well, when we get home, we will have a banquet for everyone who's helping you out. Daddy has finished his second round of chemo, and his white count is down."

"I'm gonna send your mama home next week, so she can get us more clothes. I pretty much go around in this gown, with my backside hangin' out." Sam laughed but began to cough uncontrollably.

"Sweetie, I need to tend to Daddy. Call me in a few days, and we can do this again. It was so good to see your face."

"For me too, Mama. I miss you both so much and pray every night for a speedy return." Hannah looked at her father. She knew he wouldn't be home any time soon. "Good-bye, I love you both so much."

Hannah sat for a while longer trying to make sense out of all that had happened. Her father wasn't supposed to be so sick. She'd always thought he was the family's strength but realized her mother was the glue that kept them all together. How she wanted to feel her mother's arms around her, telling her that everything would be all right. The need to cry was overwhelming, and she finally allowed the tears to flow freely.

†

Hannah pulled in front of the house. She saw the truck parked there and Mick leaning against it with her arms folded. With her emotions at the edge of out of control, Hannah took a deep breath before getting out. "What the hell are you doing here? Get out and don't come back, Mick."

"I'm not leaving until you let me explain."

"Not interested." Hannah brushed past Mick, who tried to touch her. "Get your hands off of me and get out." She heard the vitriol in her own voice and tried to rein it in.

"You have to listen to me, Hannah. She's not my wife. We're divorced."

"I don't need to listen to a damn thing you have to say. On the sidewalk outside your house, you told me you *were* married. Now you're not? Yeah right." Hannah climbed the stairs then turned around at the top to face Mick. "Get this straight," she said between gritted teeth. "I don't believe a word that comes out of your mouth. You already lied to me or my parents. You told them you grew up in Colorado and told me it was Waco."

"If you'll only let me explain, I can make it right. Just give me a chance," Mick pleaded.

"Get out." Hannah turned and stormed into the house." They never locked the door, but she did this time.

Fear gripped Hannah the next morning. The fight with Mick had really shook her. Although the house was locked up, she knew it wouldn't be hard to jimmy the locks. Silently she listened to see if she heard any noise that shouldn't be there. Nothing. She pulled on her jeans and shirt but carried her boots. With soft steps, she walked into the front room. A knock on the door startled her. With caution, she went to the front door and pulled back the sheer curtain. She let out a big breath.

"Nelly, come on in."

"Good morning, Hannah. I'm a bit early today. I hope it's okay."

"Of course it is. You're always welcome. Mama always told me that you are the nicest person she knows." Hannah patted the older lady's shoulder. "Can I get you some coffee or tea, Nelly?"

"No thanks. I need to collect the eggs and be off. It's my bread making day. I've got it rising, so I can't leave it alone for too long." Nelly grinned. "I brought you a surprise."

"Really? What?"

"You'll see, while I gather the eggs."

"Well, come on then. I'll help you."

When they stepped outside, a large golden dog ran up to them.

"This is Oscar. He needs a home. I figure, since you're out here all alone, he'll keep you company and maybe chase the bad guys off." Nelly laughed. "Not that we have many around these parts."

Hannah knelt down and scratched the dog's head. "He seems friendly."

"He is. Showed up at my house a week ago and stayed. I am too old to care for him properly. I thought you and he would get along just fine."

"I'll give him a try." Hannah smiled. "Our last dog died when I was little. For some reason, we never got another one."

They gathered the eggs, and Hannah got acquainted with Oscar as Nelly pulled away. Another plume of dust was coming toward the house. Hannah instantly recognized Mick's truck. She hurried inside and locked the door and noted the time. Mike Bonus, who owned the section next to theirs, would arrive soon to help with knifing the weeds.

Through the window, she could see Mick get out of her pickup. Oscar who was usually a friendly dog, stood with his nose up and ears back while aggressively barking at the intruder.

"I know you're in there, Hannah. Come out so we can talk." Mick repeatedly screamed through the closed door. Oscar became more agitated kept barking louder. Another pickup came up the road and stopped next to Mick's.

Mick got back in her old truck and drove away. Oscar ran to the newcomer, wagging his tail. Hannah's shoulders relaxed. Oscar would work out just fine. He'd be her protector.

Later that night, Hannah tossed and turned. She'd really thought that Mick would be the one to heal her heart and bring her happiness. *Wrong.* Her hand snaked over to the bedside table. She picked up her phone and dialed a number. "Mama, I need you."

CHAPTER □ EVENTEEN

"Hannah sweetheart, what's the matter? Are you sick?" Ada asked.

"Mama, it's Mick."

"Okay, what about her? Was she in an accident? What is so awful that you'd call me at midnight?"

"You remember how I told you that I thought we had something real?"

"Yes..." Ada drew the word out in a careful tone that sounded like a question.

"I went over there after supper yesterday, so I could use her Internet to Skype with you and Daddy." Hannah sucked in a trembling breath. "I was so happy that I was going to see you and Daddy. Although I have to admit some of my good mood was because I'd see her."

"Okay.... So, what happened to change that?"

"When I got there, another woman answered the door. She told me she was Mick's wife. How could she lie to me about that, Mama? She said she didn't have anyone." Hannah lost the battle and her tears fell.

"What did she say? Was there an explanation?"

"She chased after me, begging me to let her explain." Hannah blew out a breath and reigned in her tears. "I didn't want to hear anything she had to say. I just got in my truck and left."

"And is that all?"

"She showed up at our house, screaming that I needed to listen."

"Did you speak to her then?"

"No. Nelly brought me a stray she found, and I'm pretty sure Mick thought twice about coming toward me."

"You have a dog?"

"Yeah. His name is Oscar. With him around, I feel safe."

"Then I'm glad you have him. Just don't tell your daddy."

"Why?"

"We had a dog, Jake. Do you remember him?"

"Yeah. He was brown, wasn't he?"

"Yes. Your daddy loved that dog.... They were best friends. One day, Jake just wasn't there, and Daddy went out to find him."

"Did he find him?"

"Yeah, the coyotes got him. After that, Daddy said we'd never have a dog again. He didn't want his kids to see what he did."

"That's horrible."

"Yes it was. Now back to your problem."

Hannah tried to take a cleansing breath and failed. "Mama, what's so wrong with me that I can't find someone who will love me and let me love her?"

"Sweetie, I will be home next Tuesday. We'll figure it out. Bo will pick me up at the airport on Monday, then drive me home on Tuesday."

"Mama, I know you have your plate full being with Daddy, but I need you."

"I know. I'll be there in four days and a wake up."

Hannah laughed at the comment. When she was growing up and her parents went away, her mama would say the same thing.

"Will you be okay until then?" Ada asked.

"Yes," Hannah said with a shaky breath. "I'm sorry for being selfish. How is Daddy doing?"

"He's holding his own. Like I said, his white count is cooperating, and that is what we want to see. Now, I want you to blow your nose and dry your eyes, then get some sleep."

"What if she comes back?"

"You can do nothing, or you can listen to what Mick has to say. Otherwise, you will never know. You understand, don't you?"

"Yes," Hannah whispered. "I didn't like it when Charlie didn't give me an explanation."

"Exactly. Make sure the house is buttoned up. Now that you have Oscar to alert you if she comes back, you can go to sleep knowing you are safe."

"Okay. Thanks, Mama. I'll see you in four days and a wake up." Hannah hung up knowing that the closest neighbor would never hear someone breaking in, but Oscar would.

✝

Hannah went into town to pick up some milk, bread, and orange juice. Her mother was due home soon. Curiosity got the better of her, and she drove by Mick's house. There was a *For Sale* sign in the small front yard. "Now there's a surprise," she muttered. "More evidence that she was lying to me all along." Ashamed that she'd allowed herself to be duped, Hannah sped away toward home.

Every inch of the house got scrubbed, including the refrigerator and oven. In a matter of hours, her mother would be back home. Hannah was concentrating on keeping her emotions under control. She needed her mother's grounding presence. She paced the porch, obsessively, eyes directed into the distance. Finally, a hint of dust floated in the air. The dust cloud came closer, and her heart beat faster. Hannah wiped away the tears that trickled out of her eyes.

When Bo's car pulled up and stopped, Hannah ran to the rider's side and opened the door. She hugged her mother close to her. "I'm so glad you're home." Mother and daughter walked arm in arm into the house.

"How I've missed being here," Ada said, as Bo came through the door carrying two suitcases. Hannah pointed at the luggage.

"Does that mean you're here for an extended stay?"

"No, I leave next Monday. Bo is going to stay here and help you until Friday. When he leaves, Mack will come and stay until I need to leave on Monday for my flight back to Houston."

"Oh." Hannah could hear the disappointment in her voice and hugged her mother. "I'll take you for as long as I can. Thanks, Bo, for staying to help out away from your home and family in Amarillo. As I've found over the last month farming alone isn't easy. Luckily, we have great neighbors who are helping me out."

"I know, Sis. Daddy told us to git our butts down here and help. Between me and the help from our friends and neighbors, you should be able to rest up until next Monday."

"Thank you. I can use the time to get my energy back." Hannah hugged her brother. "Thank you, Bo," she said into his shoulder. Hannah tamped down her emotions and let go. "Come on, let's get these bags in the bedrooms. Mama, can I bring you a glass of tea?"

"That will be delightful. No one makes tea as good as you. You know the exact amount of sweetener I like." Ada grinned. "One teaspoon."

That night the three of them and Oscar sat on the front porch, enjoying the calmness that was home.

"It was so nice of Maudie to let us use her Internet and back room to speak with Daddy," Ada said.

"How does he look tonight, compared to when you left?" Bo asked.

Ada shook her head. "About the same. He had a real hard time with the chemo. It seems to take him a long time to get his head back to what it was." She scrunched her face. "Just in time for the next round."

"What do the doctors say?" Hannah tried to keep the tremor out of her voice and failed.

"The same thing—give it time. Right now, they're watching his blood...the white cells I think...so the count doesn't go too high. They check that the chemo is lowering the number." Ada took Hannah's hand. "This is not going to be a quick fix. It's going to take time. At least three months but maybe longer. There was some talk about stem cells, but I'm not sure what that is all about."

"We can call Doc Evans tomorrow and get his ideas on what stem cells are or do." Hannah squeezed her mother's hand. "Together we are strong, and we will give all of that strength to Daddy to fight this and win."

"Amen," Ada said. "I always knew our family would be there for each other."

They sat in companionable silence for a spell.

"Who is coming tomorrow and at what time?" Bo asked.

"Tomorrow is John Buck. He usually gets here early, around seven."

"John. Wow that's a name from the past." Bo laughed. "We had some good times." He cleared his throat. "Guess I need to get some sleep, so I am ready to work in the morning." Bo got up, kissed his mother's cheek, and then ruffled Hannah's hair before going inside.

"It's been a long day for me too," Ada said. "It will be nice to sleep where it's quiet. I've missed that." She kissed Hannah's other cheek. "I'll make you breakfast tomorrow."

"I'd like that," Hannah said. "Sleep well, Mama."

Once her mother went inside, Hannah looked out over the horizon at the sky and saw a shooting star. "Please keep my Daddy safe," she whispered.

The next morning, Hannah went into the kitchen and felt the sensation of déjà vu. Her mother was standing at the stove flipping pancakes. "Good morning." She walked behind her mother and gave her a hug. "I almost forgot what it looks like with you at the stove."

"I missed you too, sweetie. Go ahead and sit down. I've got a stack for you."

"This is a welcome surprise." Hannah slathered butter on the cakes, then poured syrup over them. When she cut into the stack and took the first bite, she groaned. "Oh, this is heaven. I need your recipe, so I can cook some for myself."

Ada laughed. "I'll gladly give you my secret recipe, but I seriously doubt you'll use it."

"Hey, I might just give it a try." Hannah took another bite. "Oh, these are the best you've ever made, Mama."

"I'll freeze some for you."

"Thank you."

"Do I smell Mama's famous pancakes?" Bo strolled into the kitchen.

"Take a seat. I've got some ready for you."

After breakfast, Hannah was at the sink, washing the breakfast dishes with her mother. "How are you doing here?" Ada asked.

"The truth?"

"Of course."

"It's harder than I imagined to run the place by myself. If it wasn't for the neighbors helping me, I don't think I'd make it, Mama. How did Daddy do this all by himself?"

"He had help from the boys and you. Before that, I helped him."

"What am I going to do, Mama? I'm not sure I can do it." Hannah blew out a breath and bowed her head. "I don't want to let Daddy down."

"Sweetie, you could never let him down. He adores you. If you need advice, why not give him a call and talk to him about it. That would give him something else to think about besides the treatments he's getting."

"That's a great idea. I can actually help him get better."

"Yes, you can. Just remember, to keep your voice upbeat. He slips into depression sometimes, so never let him know you're struggling."

"I will, Mama. Thank you."

Hannah heard the back door open, and Bo said, "Come on, Sis, we're burning daylight."

†

Over the visit, Hannah and her Mama took time out each day to talk. The time they spent together helped them both heal their injured souls, until they were finally able to move forward to the challenges that faced them both.

"I'm trying to stay strong for him, but it is so hard," Ada said the day before she was set to leave.

Hannah put her arm around her mother's shoulders. "It's like bein' on an emotional roller coaster, I think. Some days you're up and happy, then somethin' happens to remind you that happiness is fleeting."

"Is that how it was for you when Charlie left?" Ada asked.

"Mama, I think Daddy havin' cancer is more important than Charlie leavin'."

"Not necessarily. We were all blindsided by Daddy's illness, just as Charlie blindsided you." Ada hugged her daughter. "What you went through and are still going through puts you right there next to me on that roller coaster."

"How will we get through this, Mama?" Hannah looked at a picture of the family on the wall. "No matter how hard I try, I just can't seem to turn the corner. I tried with Mick, and that was a disaster."

"What you do is hold your head high and get on with your life. You leave the past behind."

"Easier said than done, but I will give it a try. In return, you have to have positive thoughts about Daddy gettin' better." Hannah looked into her mother's eyes. "He *will* get better."

"And your heart will mend."

The week seemed to fly by. Before Hannah knew it, her mother was packing her suitcase. "I'm going to miss you, Mama." Hannah hefted the full suitcase. "Did you pack a load of bricks?"

Ada laughed. "No. We need clothes. We didn't take much when we went to the hospital."

Hannah was taking the suitcase to Mack's truck, with her mother close by. She saw Oscar running alongside Nelly's truck until it stopped. The older woman hurried over to them.

"Glad I got you before you left, Ada." Nelly hugged her. "No worries about your girl. I will take good care of her."

"Thank you, Nelly. That does ease my worry." Oscar ran up to them. "And thank you for this addition." Ada scratched his head.

"I knew they'd be a perfect match."

Ada hugged her longtime friend.

"I do have some bad news," Nelly said.

"Oh? What is that?"

"Martha Gaines passed yesterday."

Ada looked at her watch. "I won't make my flight if I go see Bobby now." She turned to Hannah. "I need you to help me out. Please go to the viewing and the funeral and represent me and your daddy."

"Mama." Hannah gave her a pleading look. "Please don't ask me to do that."

"I need you to do that for me. They are our friends, and we need to acknowledge their loss."

"But, Mama—"

Ada leaned in and hugged her daughter. "Please, do it for me. Remember what we talked about," she whispered. "I know you can. Maybe this will give you the closure you've needed all these years."

Hannah relented, "Okay, for you, I will do it."

"Thank you, sweetheart. Please pick up a prayer card for me."

"I will." Hannah kissed her mother one more time, before helping her into the car. "Drive safe, Mack."

"Will do, Sis."

"Thanks for all your help."

"No problem."

Hannah and Nelly watched the car disappear down the road. "Come on, Nelly, I'll help you collect the eggs."

After Nelly left, Hannah sat on the porch, rocking slowly in her great-grandfather's rocker. Oscar was lying next to her, and he gave her comfort. She wasn't alone. A question ran through her mind like a crawl line on the television. *How can I go to that funeral and remain sane?*

CHAPTER EIGHTEEN

The black, silk shirt fit Hannah's body perfectly, and she polished her boots on the leg of her black slacks. She took a deep breath before walking into the church. The last pew was completely empty and allowed her to scan the church to see who was there.

The doors closed, and Pastor Webster took his place at the lectern. The organist began playing "Abide with Me." The song was one of Hannah's favorites and she sang along. "Shine through the gloom and point me to the skies..." The words always gave her hope. She closed her eyes and let peace envelope her. *I can do this.*

The music stopped and Pastor Webster began to speak. Hannah tuned him out until she heard, "Martha left behind her loving husband Bobby, son Bobby Jr., and daughter Charlene. They will be in the vestibule after the interment to receive everyone. Lunch will be provided by the women's auxiliary." Peace vanished.

Hannah could see people talking to the family, but she couldn't get a look at them from where she was standing. She watched, as the coffin was rolled down the middle aisle of the church. Suddenly, she couldn't catch her breath and could feel her heart pounding in her chest. A hand took hers and a soft voice said, "In through your nose out through your mouth. Calm down. I know you can do it, sweetheart." She looked toward the voice and saw no one. "Mama?" She looked back and saw the family following the coffin. Charlie's dark eyes were focused on her.

Someone slid in next to Hannah. "You're doing a great job," Nelly whispered. "Once we pay our condolences and go to the luncheon, you can leave."

"I don't think I can do that." Hannah shook her head. "I just can't."

"Sure you can. You ran that farm all by yourself. This is nothing compared to that." Nelly put her hand in Hannah's elbow. "We will see Martha laid to rest, then go to the meal in her honor."

Hannah shrugged.

"You can do it. I'll be right there by your side."

"Why would you do that, Nelly? Did my mother ask you to?"

Nelly only shrugged. "All those years ago, when you and Charlie were going to school, I could see the love you shared. It was unmistakable. Don't give up on that or run away, Hannah. Ask her the question you need answered. Who knows, you might be surprised. Come on, let's go."

"How do you know that?"

"Your mama and I had a long discussion last week." Nelly winked. "I am now officially your stand-in mother."

Hannah nodded at the older woman, who had always been in her life. "I like the sound of that."

†

Hannah, with Nelly by her side, waited in line to express her sympathies for the loss of wife and mother. She held out her hand. "I'm sorry for your loss, Mr. Gaines. My parents send their well wishes and love."

"Thank you, Hannah. How is your father doing?"

"As well as can be expected. Even though it's been a little over a month, it is still the early days. He has a long road ahead of him."

"Please let both your parents know that I am thinking of them and praying for your daddy's recovery."

Hannah and Nelly moved on to express their sympathies to Bobby Jr. and his wife. The time arrived, and Hannah found herself face to face with Charlie. She didn't look a day older. Her long, black hair was pulled back into a messy bun, and her eyes still held the sparkle Hannah always saw. Charlie was even more beautiful than the memory Hannah had held onto for years.

"Please accept my condolences for the passing of your mother," Hannah said in a clipped tone, refusing to look Charlie in the eyes.

"Thank you. I appreciate you being here." Charlie's voice was so soft that Hannah had to lean in to hear.

"No problem."

"Can we get together tomorrow? I need to talk with you so I can explain," Charlie whispered.

"I think you said it all in the one letter you sent to me since you left."

"Please," Charlie reached out and touched Hannah's arm. "Hannah, let me explain."

The touch was more than she could manage. She couldn't stop the memories from flooding back. Hannah had heard the words 'I can explain' more than enough times from Mick. But Charlie was standing before her, offering the explanation she'd longed to hear. She suddenly could feel a rush of dread devour her. "I can't do this," she said before rapidly walking away and heading for the exit.

"You cannot go yet." Nelly had come out of nowhere.

"Sure I can. I did as my Mama asked me to do. I went to the funeral and offered my sympathies to the family. That is all I needed to do."

"You still need an answer, Hannah. From what I heard, she wants to give that to you," Nelly said softly. "Give her a chance. You never know what will come from just listening."

"I've done all the listening I care to, Nelly. At this moment, I have nothing left to give. If you'd like a ride home, I am leaving now." Hannah scanned the room and took a quick mental note of who was there. She left without a backward glance.

"Wait for me," Nelly said.

Just as Hannah got to her truck, Charlie came up next to her, all out of breath.

"Hannah please, can we talk? There's so much I need to tell you. So much you don't know."

"No, I don't think I have anything to say to you. Your one letter and your actions told me everything I needed to know."

"Look, I know I hurt you—"

"Hurt me?" Hannah's eyes flashed wide. She glared at Charlie. "You didn't hurt me, Charlie—you destroyed me." Hannah was shouting. She didn't care if anyone was looking her way. "Let's go, Nelly, I've got work to do." Nelly went around the truck and got in.

"Hannah, please." Charlie followed her to the truck door. "Here, take this." She shoved what looked like a journal through the open window, into Hannah's hand. "You'll see why I did what I did. It's all in there."

Hannah fought with the urge to throw the journal back in Charlie's face. "Fine." She handed the book to Nelly, who was buckling her seatbelt. With the key in the ignition, Hannah took one last look. She saw tears pooling in Charlie's eyes and brushed at her own.

Nelly patted her arm. "It will work out. I promise. Trust in what your heart tells you."

"I don't think I can do this." She pointed at the journal. "Please take that with you."

"I can't do that. If I leave with it, you'll never have closure." Nelly lifted Hannah's chin. "Closure is what you want, isn't it?"

Hannah nodded.

"Then you really have no choice." Nelly held up the journal. "Charlie told you that all the answers are in here. You need to be brave enough to face the unknown and get those answers."

"I'll think on it." Hannah stopped near Nelly's house.

Nelly looked at Hannah intently. "Ever since my George died, I've realized that, sometimes, you have to take a chance. Without risk, there's no possibility. Do you understand what I'm saying?" Nelly asked, as she opened the truck door.

"Yes." Hannah pursed her lips and furrowed her brow. "You're telling me to forget everything and just jump in with two feet."

"Exactly." Nelly reached over and gently squeezed Hannah's arm. "Courage, my dear, courage. Thanks for the ride."

Once she made sure that Nelly was inside of her house and safe, Hannah headed toward the farm. She noticed the journal on the seat. "How did she do that without me seeing?" She grumbled, "When I get home, I'll burn the damn thing and be done with it." Hannah shook her head. "What a coward I am. Why do I always run away from anything emotional?" The empty truck didn't answer.

An image of Charlie came to mind, and it was almost more than she could bear. Did she want to let Charlie go? If she did, would not knowing the answers eventually consume her being, as it had for so many years? *The only person who controls your life, girly is you. It's up to you and no one else how your life will go.* "Wise words, Daddy. It's time to stop being a coward and face the truth."

†

Oscar followed Hannah to her bedroom, and she changed into her jeans and a long-sleeve shirt. There still was work to be done. Three hours of sunlight would be enough time to clean out the chicken coops that she'd been ignoring for way too long. The odor permeated the air almost to the house. That chore was what she needed to clear her mind of the morning's events. She scooped up the nasty old straw and listened to the chickens cackling their objections to her interference. Soon her labor did the trick. Her only thought was to hurry up and get done. She still needed to feed Oscar, who she saw was waiting by the door. He let her know it was time to call it a day.

After a shower and clean clothes, Hannah rummaged through the refrigerator to find something for supper. She smiled when she saw a foil-covered plate with her name on it. Hannah had forgotten that her mother had fixed a few plates ahead. There was a note taped to the foil.

H, when you eat this feel my love for you. There is nothing that love can't conquer. Mama.

She was drained and needed those simple words to make her heart swell with love. "You're right, Mama. Once I get my head around everything, I'll read that journal and see what Charlie has to say." Hannah yawned. She stood with great effort and put the meal back in the refrigerator. She headed toward her bedroom, intending to take a short nap. She was both physically and mentally exhausted. Mechanical motions pulled off her clothes, before she flopped down on her bed and pulled the covers over her. Oscar came into the room and jumped up on the bed. Hannah put an arm around him, comforted by his warmth, and fell into a deep sleep.

A loud pounding on the door sent Oscar barking and had Hannah sitting up straight in her bed. She was naked and had no idea why. The knocking continued, and she hurried to pull on her jeans. She hastily tried to button her shirt while hurrying to the door.

"Nelly? Why are you early?"

"I'm not. It's nine, and your help is already at work."

"Oh crap, I overslept. I was tossing and turning all night. Come on in and grab a cup of coffee. I'll will be with you in a few minutes."

"Already had my coffee. I'll just go ahead and gather the eggs." Nelly headed for the back door. "When I get back, you can make us both some eggs."

"Sure, I can do that." Hannah washed up and changed her clothes. When she returned to the kitchen, Nelly was coming in the door. "Good, you're done." Hannah smiled at the woman who was fast becoming a grounding force for her. "How would you like your eggs, Nelly?"

"Scrambled," Nelly said. "I'll fix the toast." Soon they were sitting at the table, eating their eggs and toast and drinking orange juice.

"Nelly, I'm sorry for how I spoke to you yesterday. Seeing Charlie again, after all this time, caught me off guard."

"I know that, Hannah." Nelly patted her hand. "I don't need an apology, but Charlie does."

"You don't know the whole story, Nelly. She destroyed me."

"You don't know the whole story either," Nelly said softly. "Did you ever think that sometimes leaving is the only option?"

"She left me without a word and later sent me a note saying, 'get out of my life.'" Hannah rubbed her face with her hand. "I would have done anything for her. All she had to do was tell me why, and I would have done whatever she wanted. That stupid note was all I got."

Nelly shrugged. "Maybe she couldn't tell you."

Hannah looked at Nelly, realizing she knew more than she was letting on. "Out with it, Nelly. What do you know?"

"Have you read the journal Charlie gave you?"

"No, and I'm not sure I will. I'm not in the frame of mind to do that."

"Hannah," Nelly said, "It will take time, but I know reading that journal might set you free."

"I'm not sure about that."

"I thought you wanted answers. You have them handed to you and you choose not to find out?"

"I don't want to say something that I'll regret later." She eyed Nelly. "I can tell there's something else you want to say."

"I wasn't sure how you felt after seeing her yesterday, but I can see how you feel today. You know anger is a horrible replacement for someone you love."

"Right now, I don't know how I feel. Was I glad to see her? Of course I was. She's the love of my life and probably always will be. But she left me without a word. How can I ever trust her again?"

"Trust your heart. It won't steer you wrong. I have something for you." Nelly reached into the pocket of her jeans and took out a piece of paper that she laid it on the table. "Well, I'm off to distribute the eggs. I'll see you in a few days." Nelly pulled Hannah into a hug and whispered, "If you ever just want to talk, I'm a good listener." She let go and smiled. "Thanks for the breakfast."

Hannah listened to the door closing after Nelly left. Oscar came bounding into the kitchen, dancing around. "Are you hungry, boy?" She scraped the leftover eggs into the dog's bowl and added some dry food. "There you go, buddy." Hannah watched her dog eat until she finally relented and reached across the table for the folded paper. She opened it and read...

H, hopefully you've read some of my journal and understand that I had no choice. I'll be at our special place at eleven, if you'd like to meet, or anywhere else that you want. Here's my cell number 888-976-0445.

Hannah replied by texting. Maudie's' this afternoon at 1.

It didn't take long for her phone to beep that she had a reply. *I'll be at Maudie's at 1 this afternoon. C*

CHAPTER NINETEEN

Hannah climbed into her truck. Charlie's journal was still on the seat. She picked it up and put it in the glove compartment. "I'll read that later." She ground her teeth while wondering why she was going to meet the one person who broke her heart into a million pieces. *I need closure, that's why.* With that thought, she sped off to town and her meeting with Charlie.

Maudie's was crowded. The only free table was by the front window. Hannah shook her head and glanced around the full room, wondering why she wanted to come here with the whole town watching. *Mistake.* She claimed the table and internally growled. The last thing she wanted to do was sit there in front of the whole town talking to Charlie. For the next ten minutes, she kept her eyes looking out the window, while scanning the room occasionally to see if anyone was leaving. No one was. She saw Charlie walking quickly toward the café. When the door opened, Hannah finally let out the breath she'd been holding.

"I'm here at last," Charlie said with a subdued look. "Sorry I'm late. I ran into Mrs. Maybury, and she wanted to offer her condolences. It seems that everywhere I go in town, the same thing happens." She looked around. "This place hasn't changed has it? Did you order?"

Hannah shook her head. "I didn't know what you wanted." She did though, for Charlie always wanted a malted when they came there in the past.

A nervous boy, who couldn't be older than sixteen, came to the table. "What can I getcha?"

"I just want sweet tea," Hannah said.

"I'll have a chocolate malted." Charlie said.

They sat silently until their drinks arrived and for a few beats after that. "When will you be going back?" Hannah finally asked.

"I'm not. I've taken a sabbatical." Charlie sucked in a breath. "I need to fix things here before I can go back."

"Things? Am I missing something? Does it have to do with your mother's will?" Hannah was systematically shredding the paper napkin she held in her hands. She knew exactly what Charlie was saying, but she wasn't going to be the first one to acknowledge it.

Charlie let out what sounded like an exasperated breath, before she pointed a finger and waved it between them. "I need to fix us."

"There isn't an us anymore, Charlie. You walked away. Remember." Hannah tried to tamp down her rising anger.

"Obviously, you didn't read my journal, or you didn't believe what you read. Which is it?"

"I haven't read it yet," Hannah said softly. "Since my daddy got sick, I've been running the farm alone, except for a few neighbors who used to come by to help me. Right now, they have too much to do at their own places, so I call if I need them." Hannah lifted a shoulder and blew out a breath. "To tell you the truth, I'm afraid of what I might find out about your rejection of me."

"Rejection? No. No. It's quite the opposite, Hannah. I am hoping that reading the journal that I've kept since the day we met will heal your heart and make you understand why I had to leave." Charlie reached across the table and put her hand over Hannah's. "I left to save you. I loved you then, and I still do now."

Hannah pulled her hand away. "You have a funny way of showing love. All I've known from you since you left is pain and unhappiness."

"No. That isn't at all the way I wanted it to be. The reason I—"

"Well, well lookie who's here. It didn't take long for you to find someone else did it?" Mick said. "And here I was thinkin' that we'd be together forever."

"Get lost, Mick. You're not wanted here." Hannah saw the two men at the table next to them shake their heads and whisper something. *Great that's all I need. People talking about me.*

"Aren't you gonna introduce us?" Mick held out her hand to Charlie. "I'm Mick Hendricks, and Hannah here is my girl."

"I am not!"

Charlie shook Mick's hand.

"Charlene Gaines. Nice to meet you, Ms. Hendricks."

The loud scrape of Hannah's chair along the wooden floor almost covered her growl. When she saw the diners around her turn away when she looked at them, she balled her fingers. She wouldn't allow Mick try to get her claws into Charlie.

"Call me Mick. Everyone does." Mick took a step toward Charlie.

Hannah stepped in front of Mick. "Get the hell out of here right now, or I will throw you out." She'd tried to keep her voice low, but the dangerous rumble had people in the café looking at them again. She could see hands over mouths, disguising their whispers. Hannah knew them all and was certain some of them had speculated about her and Charlie, or her and Mick. For a moment, Hannah considered she was being paranoid before she leveled Mick with a hateful gaze.

Mick flinched.

"Get out. Now," Hannah said between gritted teeth.

"I'm not done," Mick whispered then turned to Charlie. "Nice to meet you, Charlene. I'm sure we will meet again." Mick winked at her and left.

"It looks like my leaving wasn't all that devastating to you." Charlie sounded defeated. "I can't believe how you treated that woman. You never used to be that way, Hannah."

Hannah sat back down. "Well, that all changed when you left."

"How long before you fell into her arms?"

"I didn't fall into anyone's arms. That never happened. I helped her fix up her grandpa's house so she could sell it. I'd been so lonely for so long that I needed to move on and stop thinking about you. I dated her twice that's all. We shared a few kisses. I could never convince my heart that she was you," Hannah said.

"Do you really think I'd fall for that story? That you were celibate for all these years?"

"Yes, because it is true. Besides, you walked out on me. What did you want me to do? Become a nun and build a shrine to you?" Hannah let out a small laugh. "I bet you had a date and a kiss if not more."

"I did not. Not one date. Not one kiss. All I thought of was you," Charlie said in a low ominous voice.

"Yeah, right."

"Read the damn journal, Hannah, so you know exactly what happened and why." Charlie got up and hurried out of the café.

Hannah sat at the table in Maudie's for a while, nursing her tea and trying to wrap her mind around what had happened. Yes, she was still angry and hurt by how Charlie had disappeared without a word. Her Mama always told her to go sit in a corner and make up her mind about what she wanted. She whispered, "I need to read that journal, the sooner the better."

"Did you want something more?" the young server asked.

She looked around the café and saw that almost everyone had left. She let out a sigh of relief. *No town's folk watching me now.* The café closed at three, and she saw that it was almost that time. "No. Sorry, I didn't keep track of the time. I'm going now." Hannah dropped a decent tip, then left the café. Once outside, she saw Mick leaning against her truck.

"It's about time," Mick said. "I thought you'd be in there forever, licking your wounds." She grinned. "I saw her storm out. Boy did she look pissed."

"Get off my truck." Hannah got inside and started the engine.

Mick opened the rider's door and got in. "I'll go home with you and help you get over her."

"Get out," Hannah barked.

"Come on, babe, you know you want it."

"Won't your wife miss you?"

"We have an open marriage. We are there for each other when the other needs some TLC." Mick laughed. "Believe me, you are a source of frustration for me. I had to call her to come give me some release."

"You need to get your stories straight, Mick. First, you're married, then divorced, and now in an open marriage. Which is it? Did you grow up in Waco or Colorado?" Mick just glared at her. "You know, Mick, not a single person I've talked to can't remember your grandpa ever having you live with him. Is that another one of your lies? Did you ever tell me the truth about anything? Was he even your grandpa?"

"I've only ever told you the truth." Hannah saw a shifty look on Mick's face.

"You know, what occurred to me, Mick, is how you practically knew the exact value of the antiques your grandpa left. It was awfully convenient that you found his book with the values. I'm pretty sure I looked through all the drawers and never saw it." Hannah looked directly into Mick's eyes. "Was he even your grandpa?"

"You take that back," Mick demanded. "The only thing you should understand, Hannah, is that I have you now. Your old heart throb is gone, and I intend to take you as mine."

"That will never happen. Now get out of my truck, or I will call Sherriff Morgan to come and arrest you for harassment. Maybe I'll clue her in on all your contradictions."

Mick put her hand on the handle and pushed the door open with a squeal. "Your loss. Maybe I'll hunt down your Charlene and see if I can soothe her. I can't be the only one you've been a tease to."

"You go near her, Mick, and I will make sure that you regret it. Is that clear?" Hannah watched Mick walk away without another word, then closed her eyes. When she opened them again, she stared at the glove compartment for moment. "I can't believe how tired I am." She put the truck in gear and headed slowly toward home. She needed a decent meal. She'd take her frustrations out on the weeds, then give Oscar a good brushing.

CHAPTER TWENTY

After an hour of chopping at weeds with a hoe, Hannah had finally given up and gone to bed. When the first tendrils of sun made their way into her bedroom, Hannah was surprised that she felt refreshed. Oscar came bounding into the room and jumped on the bed. "Get down. It's time to have breakfast and do some work." As she dressed, memories of Charlie crept into her mind and try as she might, she couldn't get rid of them. "I don't have time for that nonsense. I have a cotton farm to work."

Hannah put all she had into her labors for the entire day, thereby keeping Charlie on the edges of her mind and not up front and present. At the end of the long workday, Hannah was sitting on the side of her bed when her phone rang.

"Hi, Mama, what's up."

"Hannah, sweetheart, I need you to come to Houston right away."

"Mama, what's wrong? Is Daddy okay?"

"I don't know. The doctors won't tell me. They said to wait for the test results. How many more tests can they give him?"

"Okay, Mama, I'll be there as soon as I can. If I can't get a flight, I'll drive."

"Please be careful. I need to call the boys."

"I'll let you know when I'm close."

"I love you, Hannah. Be safe."

After Hannah ended the call, she dialed Nelly's number. "Hi, Nelly, it's Hannah. I need a big favor."

"Sure. You know I'll do anything for you."

"My mama called. Daddy, apparently, has taken a turn. She needs Mack, Bo, and me to be there."

"What can I do?"

"Would you come and stay here with Oscar until I get back? There are still some of the guys who come and go to help me, but not as many and...well, I don't think there is anyone around who knows more about cotton farming than you. I can still remember my dad saying that you and Henry made quite a team."

"That we did." Nelly let out an audible breath.

"I know," Hannah said softly.

"Are you flying or driving?"

"Flying if I can get a ticket. I wanted to call you first to make sure someone knew I was gone."

"I will stay at your place and make sure the farm keeps running until you get back. Now go book a flight and pack your bags. I'll get a few things and come over there. If you're gone, I'll let myself in."

"Thank you so much, Nelly. Oh, Oscar will need feeding. He stays in the house at night. Safer that way."

"I'll take care of him. Now, scoot and go. Your mama needs you."

†

Hannah paid the taxi driver and grabbed her backpack. She rushed into M.D. Anderson and confirmed the room number, then hurried to the elevator bank. She waited impatiently for one to open. When she arrived at her father's room, she sucked in a deep breath.

"You're here," Ada said hugging her. "They had him in isolation, because his immune system needed protection and they didn't want to take a chance of infection, at least that's what I think the doctor said. I was so afraid, but it now looks like he has rallied."

Bo and Mack surrounded their mother and Hannah in a group hug.

"I'm sorry that I got you all to come down here—"

"Mama, we said we'd be here for you, no matter when or where," Mack said. "Did the doctors say anything else?"

"Yes, and that is the best part. I just spoke with Dr. Murray. She said that Daddy has finished his second cycle of chemo. They are now checking that all the cancer cells are gone. That means he is on his way to remission."

"That's great news, Mama," Bo said.

"That's not the best part. Dr. Murray said that as long as he continues to improve Daddy can be transferred to Texas Oncology Amarillo in a few weeks."

"Fantastic, he'll be closer to home, Mama." Hannah hugged her mother again.

"After that, they will start looking for the bone marrow donor for the transplant." Ada clasped her hands. "For the first time, I feel truly hopeful."

The room fell silent for several moments.

"Hannah, we were speaking to Mama before you got here. Me and Bo will come for a week each to help you with the farm. Now that we know he'll be coming home sooner, rather than later, we need to find out if Daddy will need a hospital bed and what other things he'll need while convalescing. Once we know that, we can fix up a room in the house for him," Mack said.

"Hey, let's not put the cart before the horse," Bo said. "Let's take care of the farm first. When we know more about Daddy coming home, we can tackle that stuff."

"Good plan," Mack said.

Hannah gave them all a perplexed look. What the hell? Now they're taking over and not even including me in the conversation. That's typical of them.

"Mama, are you hungry?"

Ada shook her head.

"You need to eat, Mama. You'll be no use to Daddy if you let yourself get sick too." Hannah said. "You will need all your strength, so take advantage of us being here now."

"You're right," Ada said. "Let's go grab a bite. Maybe, when we get back, we can see him."

†

Hannah disembarked from the plane, bypassing the luggage carousel since all she had was her backpack. The dry heat of west Texas was a welcome relief from the humidity in Houston. She walked quickly to her truck and sat with the memory of the last day at the hospital.

They were all visiting with their daddy and smiles were on everyone's face. "He looks great, don't you think?" Bo asked.

"He's better than I've seen him in a long time. We need to get the place all spruced up for his home coming," Mack said.

"Excuse me, do you two think you are going to swoop in and take over the farm?" Hannah looked at their wide eyes. "I don't think so."

"Sorry, Sis," they said in unison.

"We know you're the boss," Bo said.

Hannah smiled. It was all working out. Finally, her mind and heart were feeling lighter than they had in a long time. She searched for the parking ticket but couldn't find it. She pulled down both visors, checked the center console and the floor, and still didn't find it. When she reached across and opened the glove compartment, she sucked in a breath. The parking ticket was there along with the journal. She only took the ticket.

The loud rumble from her stomach competed with the truck's engine. Hannah pulled the pickup into the first drive-in burger place she saw and pressed the order button. The food arrived quickly, and she pushed the seat back to be more comfortable while she ate. She kept looking toward the glove compartment. It was time. She couldn't deny its pull any longer and reached across the seat to take the journal out of the glove compartment. Her fingers trembled as she opened the cover.

Today I met a girl named Hannah Gaines. WOW!!! I never met anyone like her. We talked and talked and never ran out of things to say. At times I saw her looking at me and it gave me chills. She is perfect!!!!!

I saw Hannah at school today and when our eyes met I couldn't look away. She said she'd show me how to get to my house from the bus. I didn't tell her that I already knew because I wanted to spend more time with her. She is something else.

Hannah flipped a few pages.

Today Hannah came home with me and we went to my bedroom and began to study. My mom came in and shouted at us for lying on the bed together. I was so embarrassed. Why can't she leave me alone and stop trying to interfere in my life? Hannah of course got off the bed immediately and said she needed to go home…I know she didn't…it was all because of my mother….how I hate her. Why can't she be normal like Hannah's mother???

A week later, Charlie wrote…

We hung out in the loft of the Gaines' barn today and saw her brother Mack come in with Ginger Colby. It wasn't long before they began to kiss and then he ran his hand over her butt. She of course moved but when he did it again she let him. All the time we watched Hannah held my hand and it gave me a strange feeling. It wasn't a bad feeling it was just different than I ever felt.

A knock on the pickup's window had Hannah looking up at the woman who had brought her burger. "You want anything else?" the server asked.

"Yeah, can I have another sweet tea?"

"Sure thing, sweetie. Will that be all?"

"Yes." Hannah put the journal on the seat and fished out money from her pocket. She looked around. Cars filled almost every spot. After checking the time, she realized that she had been there reading for over an hour.

"Here you are, sweetie." The woman returned and gave Hannah her drink.

Hannah paid and gave the woman a generous tip. She looked at the journal, longing to read more, but she knew it was time to go. "That'll have to wait till I get home." With the truck in gear, she backed out and headed toward home.

CHAPTER TWENTY☐ ONE

Hannah's heart skipped a beat when she turned the steering wheel to go down the road to the farm. It was the first time since her daddy got sick that she had a sense of hope. Oscar came running up to her, wagging his tail and jumping at the door.

"Down, boy." Hannah jumped out and walked toward the house. She smiled at the dog, glad that she'd taken him in when Nelly brought him to her. She welcomed the company, since he helped make the house and farm not seem so empty and lonely.

Home.

Nelly was at the door when she climbed the steps. "You're back. I wasn't expecting you for a week, at least. How's your Daddy?"

Hannah detected a look of fear on Nelly's face. "He hasn't died if that's what you're worrying about."

Nelly let out an audible sigh. "Thank you, Jesus." Grinning, she grabbed Hannah's arm and pulled her into the house. "Why did your mama need you?"

"At first she thought he'd taken a turn for the worse. By the time we got there, she'd found out that he was getting better. They're going to transfer him to Amarillo if he continues to improve."

Nelly took a step and hugged Hannah close. "That is wonderful news for your family."

"Thank you, Nelly." Hannah hugged her back before letting go. "For everything."

"Well, let me get my things together and go home."

"Won't you stay and let me fix you supper?"

"As tempting as that is, I want to get home before dark, so I can check on my kitties and make sure they have food."

"How many do you have this time?"

"I've seen seven so far. The mama cat keeps them in the barn. They're a beautiful mix of the Siamese mama and some random male that she found. The few that let me get close have blue eyes. Okay, I need to get going. I'm glad for your news. See you in a few days, Hannah."

Once she saw Nelly off, Hannah walked back inside the house and could feel her whole body relax. It appeared that her father was on the mend, although she didn't really know what that meant. Once he was transferred to Amarillo, she would have a chance to quiz the doctors about the long-term prognosis. Right then, all she wanted to do was check the mail, then go around the property on the ATV before it got too dark to see how everything was progressing.

With the Gator gassed up and running, Hannah headed toward the farthest edge of their property. Oscar ran alongside. She kept her eyes focused on the rows of cotton for anything that looked wrong. All the bolls were almost mature, and she crossed her fingers that they'd reach maturity unscathed. It was critical, between now and harvesting, that the weather stay stable. All it would take was high winds, an infestation, or freezing weather to destroy many months' work. When she got to the end of their property, Hannah was satisfied that all the fields of cotton were close to being ready for the boll puller.

A memory of a time long ago came to mind, as she sat looking out over the fields...

Charlie was holding on to the sidebar and laughing. "Faster. Go faster," she screamed, and Hannah pressed the pedal. They bumped up, down, and sideways along the rutted dirt path. When they came to a fence, Hannah turned the ATV around and stopped. She ran around to help Charlie out.

"That was amazing," Charlie screamed. "Let's do it again."

That was the moment. Hannah's hands grasped Charlie's hips and lifted her out of the ATV, and she realized her feelings for her friend were more than 'just friendship'. It took all her willpower not to kiss the luscious lips that were so close to her own. Would that be welcomed, she thought while she watched Charlie laugh.

"I need to know the truth," Hannah whispered, as she turned for the house. She knew the only way to find out the why was to read Charlie's journal. She'd been too chicken. After visiting her father, she had the strength.

With her knees pulled under her, Hannah sat on the couch and Oscar snuggled up against her. She had the journal open and had been reading for about an hour. The memories of their times together kept bubbling up, as she recalled the time in her life when she was totally happy. It had all been because Charlie was in her life.

She flipped the page and her stomach flipped too. On the page was a drawing of Hannah with a heart around the picture. She knew that Charlie liked to draw pictures of places where they'd been. She'd seen quite a few in the journal. This made her jaw drop, for it was drawn six months after they first met. "She loved me then," Hannah whispered in awe. She flicked through later pages and found more drawings of herself, each more detailed than the last. By each picture was a love poem, always ending with *I love you, Hannah*.

More determined than ever to solve the mystery of why, she forced herself to stay awake and kept reading. Sleep came. Hannah opened her eyes when Oscar started barking at whoever was pounding at the door. Sunlight was streaming through the window, and she realized she'd fallen asleep on the couch. "Who can that be?"

"It can't be Nelly she isn't due for two days." She pushed up from the couch and stretched before she headed for the door.

"What are you doing here?" Hannah shook her head.

"I said I'd come stay for a week and help you out, Sis," Bo said.

"But I told you and Mack that I really didn't need help until it was time to harvest the cotton."

"Have you forgotten that this is the time when Daddy worked on the equipment, so it will be ready in the spring?"

"Yeah, I know, but I can do all that by myself. Go back to your family, Bo." All Hannah wanted to do was have a cup of coffee and get back to Charlie's journal. When she saw the crestfallen expression on her brother's face, she sighed. "Come on in. On second thought, most of the machinery needs two people when it comes to tuning them up."

"Now you're talking sense. I hope you have the coffee ready." Bo walked inside and Oscar greeted him. "I heard him barking when I knocked. When did you get a dog?"

"A while back. He showed up at Nelly's place, and she thought I needed company. So here he is."

"What's his name?"

"Oscar."

Bo was down on one knee, scratching behind Oscar's ears. "He looks a lot like the labradoodle that our neighbors have."

"That makes sense. I knew he was part lab. I just couldn't figure out the other part." Hannah smiled. "Nelly was right; he *is* great company. I'll start the coffee. Do you want some breakfast?"

"No, I had a breakfast taco in Hereford. While the coffee cooks I'll bring my things in."

"I'm glad you're here, Bo." Hannah smiled at him as he walked out the front door. She really was glad to see him. Her eyes flicked to the couch and the open journal. She'd have to make sure she went to bed early, so she could read it before she went to sleep.

176

She recalled the last entry she'd read…

Today it was my turn at school to say the announcements over the speaker system. I was so nervous and asked if Hannah could help me. 'No' was my answer. I began to speak when I saw her standing at the counter smiling at me. Later I found out that she volunteered to bring the lunch count to the office so she could be there for me. Hannah is beyond wonderful and I am the luckiest girl in school to have her as my best friend.

"I thought those days would never end," Hannah mumbled as she tucked the journal under her pillow.

†

The strippers and trucks were mostly ready for harvesting and hauling the lint to the gin. Bo and Hannah had spent four days working together. Soon, they'd begin on the tractors. Regular maintenance would prepare the equipment for plowing the fields after the first of the year.

"Hey, Sis, I'm goin' into town and pick up some grease for the tractor and a new carburetor. You wanna come along?" Bo asked.

"Daddy has a whole bucket of grease. Didn't you find it?"

"Sure did, but it's nearly empty."

Hannah frowned. "When I looked at it a month ago, the bucket was three-quarters full." She shook her head. "I bet one of the guys that came to help me took it home."

"Well if that's the price we have to pay for their help, it's probably worth it," Bo said.

"Not the point. I trusted everyone. Whoever did this stole from us." The thought crushed her.

"You don't know that, Hannah. That barn is open all the time. Anyone could have gone in there and helped themselves."

"Yeah, I guess." Her mind went over the list of everyone who'd come and helped out. She couldn't think of one that would take something without asking. "You need a new carburetor for which one?"

"The Deere. Why?"

"Daddy changed a carburetor last spring, but it was on the other tractor."

"So, do you want to come with me or not?'

"Sure, why not? Wanna stop at Maudie's or Rosie's for a real meal?" Hannah grinned.

"Not that I'm complainin' about your cookin', Sis, but a decent meal would be great." Bo chucked her on the arm. "Tomorrow, I'll do the cookin'. I make a great omelet."

"It's a deal. Come on, let's get going. Daylight is burning, and we still have a tractor to fix." Hannah tossed the truck keys to Bo. "You're driving."

Bo pulled the truck up in front of Wilkerson's Dry Goods store and turned off the ignition. "Can you think of anything else we need, besides grease and the carburetor?"

Hannah shook her head. "Nope. We won't know until we start on the big tractor."

"Come on then, let's get started. I can already taste that burger at Maudie's."

Inside Wilkerson's, Hannah watched as her brother shook hands with just about everyone. He'd always been popular at school. He made his way back to her, holding a bucket of grease.

"You'll never guess what happened." Bo said.

"They asked you to be mayor?'"

"Ha-ha, very funny. They didn't charge me for the grease."

"Why?"

"Apparently, John Buck gave them the money. He said he was in need of it and used ours, then came in here and paid for our next bucket."

"He never said anything to me about it."

"Apparently, this happened while we were in Houston." He patted her arm. "See, no one stole from us."

"Yeah. I hated to think the worst of my neighbors."

"Bad news is we have to go to the tractor graveyard for the carburetor."

"Oh joy. Just what I wanted to do today. Scrounge around old tractors and cars like the old days."

"I remember once, when Daddy took me there, I had a good time crawling over everything." Bo laughed.

Hannah shook her head. "Well come on. The sooner we find what we need, the sooner we can have lunch."

When they finally arrived at Maudie's, it was the height of the lunch crowd.

"You wanna wait or try Rosie's?" Hannah asked her brother.

"I was kinda wantin' a burger." Bo smiled. "I remember coming here with the guys and we'd all have burgers and fries. I've never had anything like it since."

"Then wait we will." Hannah stood in the doorway, surveying the diners. "I think Dale Burke is gettin' ready to leave." She grabbed Bo's hand and led him toward the table. "Howdy, Dale."

"Hannah, how's your daddy doing?"

"They're moving him to Amarillo, and that will make it easier on him and the family."

"Great news." Dale held out his hand. "Bo, how are you doin'? Been a long time since I've seen you around here."

"I'm doing good, Mr. Burke and you?"

"Good. You two want a table?"

Hannah nodded.

"Here take this one. I'm done. The special is chicken and dumplin's and it really is good." He smiled. "You take care."

"Thank you, Dale." Hannah sat in a chair with her back to the door.

"Can I get something for you to drink?" A young girl asked, as she cleared the table.

"Two sweet teas," Bo told her. "Can't wait for that burger," he said with a grin after the girl walked away.

"A bit single minded, aren't you?" Hannah laughed.

The young girl returned with the drinks. "What can I get you? The special today is chicken and dumplings."

"I'd like a medium-rare burger with all the fixin's and fries." Bo said.

"I'll have the same," Hannah replied.

After she left, Bo rubbed his hands together. "I can taste it already."

Hannah laughed. "I hope it's as good as you remember."

"Oh, it will be…it always is."

It wasn't long before they were eating in companionable silence. Occasionally, Bo let out a groan of happiness that made Hannah smile, glad that her brother was there with her.

"I knew you couldn't stay away," a low voice said.

Hannah cringed.
Mick.

CHAPTER TWENTY⬜ TWO

Hannah shook her head in disgust, not believing that Mick dared to speak to her while she was with her brother. "I thought this town got lucky and you moved away."

"I decided to stay here until you are ready to come with me to see the big wide world," Mick said with a sneer.

"I thought I made it clear that that's not ever happening. Go away, Mick. You're not wanted here, especially by me."

"We both know that's not true. I can see in your eyes that you want me." She bent down close to Hannah. "I bet right now you are remembering how it felt to be in my arms while we made love," Mick whispered.

"We both know that only happened in your mind and never in reality, Mick. Go away."

"Who is this tall and handsome fella?" Mick eyed Bo. "Don't tell me you're *bi* now."

Hannah saw the confused look on Bo's face. "My sister said you're not welcome, so why don't you leave?"

"I bet she never told you that she's into girls. Did she?" Mick grinned.

"Excuse me. Do you think I didn't know? She's my sister. Of course I'd know. Now go away." Bo scraped his chair back and started to get up. Just at that moment, a hand grasped Mick's arm, and someone began dragging her toward the door.

"I don't believe it." Hannah watched the scene, along with everyone else in Maudie's. Her mouth gaped. "Charlie?" Hannah got up. "I'll be right back and explain everything, Bo." She headed for the door and stepped outside, where Charlie had Mick backed against a brick wall.

"I don't care who you think you are, but if you keep harassing Hannah, I promise you will be sorry." Charlie gathered the front of Mick's shirt and pulled her close. "She's my friend. Always has been. She'll never be yours."

"Ha," Mick managed to say. "You walked away from her, and that makes her fair game. You didn't really think she was sitting around yearning for you, did you?" Mick choked out. "Go ahead and ask her how wet she'd get when we made love."

"That's a lie," Hannah said. "It never happened."

Mick laughed. "Sure, babe, keep telling yourself that. We both know the truth."

Hannah started toward Mick with her hand balled. Charlie stepped in front of her.

"I've got this." Charlie glared at Mick. "She's not a commodity and like I said, she definitely is not yours. Now I suggest you run along. Heed my words and stay away from

Hannah." She let go of the shirt and shoved Mick against the wall. "Now go," she growled.

"I won't be the one to be sorry. You *chica*, and your girlfriend here, will be the ones that will pay, not me. It never will be me." Mick snarled in Charlie's direction then walked away.

"Charlie, what the hell are you doing? She's unhinged or close to it. Don't ever underestimate someone like her," Hannah shouted after Mick left.

"She had no business outing you to Bo."

Hannah closed her eyes and blew out a breath. "Don't you get it? I don't know what I'd do to her if she hurt you in any way," she whispered. "I'm pretty sure it wouldn't be pretty."

"Believe it or not, Hannah, I can take care of myself."

"I know you can take care of yourself. I always knew you had my back." She looked directly into Charlie's eyes. "I miss what we had. Will you come inside and have a burger with Bo and me?"

"Are you sure?"

"Yes. Come on. We can share like we used to, and I'll get you a malted." Hannah started to go back inside the restaurant, happy that Charlie was walking alongside her.

When they got to the door, Charlie stopped. "Did you get a chance to read my journal?"

"I started reading five nights ago and fell asleep on the couch. I didn't wake up until Bo knocked on the door in the morning. I was up to the part where you were making announcements at school in eleventh grade." Hannah chuckled softly. "Everything you write comes back to me clearly, and I remember it all." She shrugged. "To tell you the truth, since Bo came, all we do is work. By eight I'm exhausted. I try to read, but I keep falling asleep."

Charlie took a step back. "Thanks for the invite for a burger, but I need to go."

"But I thought you were going to join us." Hannah could feel her heart skip a beat and land somewhere around her ankles.

Charlie ran a finger down Hannah's cheek. "I really want to join you, but you need to read all the journal before I can. When you've read it, come and find me."

"Hey, Sis, your burger is getting cold." Bo called from the door. "Hey, Charlie."

"Hey, Bo. How are you doing?"

"Good. You gonna join us?"

"No, I don't think so." Charlie smiled. "Maybe some other time."

"I'll be right there," Hannah said.

"Great." Bo went back inside the café.

"I guess I'll see you later," Hannah said to Charlie

"I hope so."

Hannah stood there watching Charlie walk away, then returned to the café. She wondered why it was so important that she read all of the journal first.

A growl escaped as they left Maudie's, and Hannah's back stiffened. Mick was leaning against the adjoining building, with her arms folded and a smirk on her face.

"Leave it." Bo took Hannah's arm. "She isn't worth it."

"I won't live my life with that woman stalking me," Hannah spat.

"Eventually, she will get tired of the game she's playing and go away."

Hannah wrestled her arm away. "Not good enough, Bo. She will go after Charlie, and I can't let that happen."

"Confrontation isn't the answer. There must be another way you can fight her without actually doing it." Bo gave her an earnest look. "Don't go down to her level. You're better than that."

Hannah stopped and smiled. "You're right. There is another way to stop her. Come on, I need you as a witness."

"Where are we goin'?"

"To see the sheriff."

Hannah parked her truck in front of City Hall, where the sheriff's offices were. She took in a deep breath and blew it out. "Come on, Bo, we can do this."

"Yes, you can," Bo answered while getting out of the truck.

They entered the office. "Hey, Marvin, hi. Is the sheriff in? I need to talk to her."

"Let me check," Marvin said.

Hannah and Bo watched the man go into an office then come back out.

"She said to go on in."

"Thanks, Marvin." Hannah gave him a smile, and she and her brother walked into the office.

Sheriff Lara Morgan looked up at them and smiled. "Well look who's here. Hannah, it's been way too long." She stood and held out her hand. After shaking hands with both Hannah and Bo, she said, "I saw Charlie a few days ago. I bet you're glad she's back."

"I am, and she's is part of my reason for being here. I've got a problem that I hope you can help me with."

"That sounds serious. What's going on?"

"You know that woman who came to town saying she was Tom Hendricks granddaughter and that he left his house to her?"

"Yeah. I've met her once or twice. From the outside it looks like she did a good job renovating that house. What about her?"

"She's threatened me and Charlie. Today, when Bo and I were having lunch at Maudie's, she made a big scene. Bo was there." She nodded at her brother, "I'm glad, because I think she may have attacked me."

"She was mighty enraged, Sheriff, and my sister is right, she looked like she was ready to take Hannah out," Bo added.

"I take it that there were more customers at Maudie's than just you two, who can verify what you've said."

"As usual, it was crowded. I'm pretty sure they all heard her." Hannah looked away. "Some of the things she said I would have rather kept to myself."

"Anything else?" the Sheriff asked.

"When I first met her, I thought it was weird that she just showed up and moved into the house. But I got to know her when I helped her with the house, so I didn't think about that anymore. Now, I'm wondering if anyone verified that she was Tom's granddaughter. Have you seen the will or deed? She said she lived here with him for six years I think, but no one seems to remember her."

The sheriff was quiet for minute, then shook her head. "No, can't say anyone verified her claim. I figured anyone who remodeled that old house like she did belonged there. Do you know differently, Hannah?"

"Well, I helped her remodel. She sold all his antiques, and I just wanted to be sure that if she is lying about who she is, I don't get mixed up in that. I also helped her sell the antiques. I introduced her to Ted Martin, and I want to make it clear that if she is an imposter, I didn't know anything about it at the time."

"Do you have any knowledge that she is an imposter?"

"Not directly. It's just things that she's said that don't add up, and she's been stalking me lately."

"Let me look into this. If I need any more information, I'll give you a call. Don't worry. I will take care of this today."

"Okay thanks, Sheriff."

Bo walked out of the sheriff's office with Hannah close behind. "I don't think she'll be bothering you again."

"You were right. There's always more than one way to resolve a problem." *I hope she didn't try to involve me in her scheme, if she isn't legitimate.*

†

That night, Hannah was sitting in the rocker on the front porch when Bo came out. He handed her a glass of tea and sat next to her.

"You've been very quiet since we left the sheriff's office."

"Lots on my mind. I'm pissed at the whole event at Maudie's. It made me feel that my only choice was to talk with the sheriff, or I'd have Mick on my back forever." Hannah looked away. "Mostly, I'm trying to figure out what to do next about Charlie.

"Wanna talk about any of it?"

"Talk about what, Bo? You were there and a witness to everything." Hannah glared at him. "That crazy bitch embarrassed me in front of all the people at Maudie's. I know most of them. You saw the altercation outside the café. Thank god everyone else didn't." She gritted her teeth. "She outed me in front of everyone. The bitch!"

"First of all"—Bo took a deep breath—"She didn't out you to me. I've known ever since high school. It was obvious when you were with Charlie."

"You knew? Why didn't you say anything?" Hannah couldn't stop her mouth from gaping open.

"Hannah, I wasn't blind. No one was. What do you want me to say? I didn't have a problem with your preferences, and no one I knew at school did either."

Hannah's eyes grew wide. "All these years, everyone knew and didn't care. Why didn't I know that? Crap, life would have been so much easier." Hannah bent her head and put her hands over her face.

"What do *you* want?"

"I want Charlie. I want to know why she just disappeared."

"Then ask her."

"I did. She gave me her journal to read."

"Did you read it?"

"Some. There's been so much going on that I don't seem to have a minute to myself."

Bo stood and patted her shoulder. "I declare that tomorrow is *Hannah's* day. I will do all the chores, and you can put your feet up and read that journal. Then put it to rest, Sis. Go forward with your life."

Hannah put her hand over Bo's and looked up at him. "Thank you, Bo."

"You bet. I'm off to bed, and I expect that you will sleep in tomorrow morning." He disappeared through the door.

Hannah once again looked out over the vast expanse before her. For the first time in what seemed like forever, she felt at peace.

†

Hannah laid in her bed reading Charlie's journal, just as she promised Bo she would. She picked up where she'd left off, with Charlie making announcements at school. It was amazing to her how Charlie had captured each day they'd spent together over four years. Sometimes the notations were short; others were longer. Each page evoked a memory of a time when they were deliriously happy.

Today we drove into town and had lunch at Maudie's. It was a hot and sunny summer day, and we went to town in hopes of finding Harvey Winkler. He is the most popular boy during the summer—he has a pool. Hannah insisted that we sit at the table by the window, so we could keep a look out for him. It didn't last long for as it was every time I am with Hannah nothing else exists. Hannah was so cute when she ordered for both of us. I asked her if ordering for me meant we were on a date. She blushed and I knew my answer. One day I will get the courage to tell her how I feel about her. I love you, Hannah.

As she read on, she knew that she was getting closer to the days before and after Charlie left. She looked at the clock radio and saw it was almost three in the morning. With a yawn, she closed the journal and put it on the bedside table. A good night's sleep is what she needed to face whatever the journal would reveal next.

While she slept, Hannah tossed and turned, occasionally punching her pillow to be more comfortable. Every memory of Charlie haunted her, as they seemed to play in a nonstop movie reel. Finally, at seven forty-five, she got up determined to finish reading. She needed to find the answer and move on with her life.

†

"I thought I told you to sleep in today. Did you forget that?" Bo asked when she walked into the kitchen.

"Bo, it's after eight, I'm usually up by six."

"Did you at least read the journal?" He put a bowl in front of her. "We're having cereal this morning. You want coffee?"

"Yes to both your questions." Hannah pulled the box of Honey Nut Cheerios toward her and poured some into her bowl.

"Did you find what you were looking for?"

"If you're asking if I know why she walked away without a word, the answer is no. It was three and I needed to sleep."

"Well, don't leave it too long." Bo placed a steaming cup of coffee in front of her. "Mike and John will be here in a little while to help me with the big tractor."

"I should be out there helping you."

"No, you shouldn't. Remember this is Hannah's day."

"If it's my day, I should do what I want, and I want to help."

"Nice try, Sis. Read the rest of the journal so you have an answer." He leveled her with a stern look. "It's time to get a life so you can stop complaining about Mack and me moving away."

191

"Fine." Hannah knew he was right. She enjoyed reliving a happier past. With each page turn, she was reconnecting with Charlie. After she finished her breakfast, she freshened her coffee and headed for her bedroom and the journal.

She put off reading with the excuse that she needed to get a shower before taking up the journal reading. She had waited a long time for the answer and reasoned that a few more minutes wouldn't hurt.

Her hands were shaking when she finally picked up Charlie's journal and turned to the page she was dreading to read. She had skimmed through the pages the night before and knew where to find the day before Charlie left. Up until then, everything she read was happy and loving. With a lump in her throat, she began to read...

Last night while Hannah and I were in her truck kissing and doing some light petting I had no idea my mother was watching us. When I went inside, she slapped me across the face. She screamed 'you nasty little slut. You're an aberration and God will punish you'. Then she pulled out my dad's old forty-five revolver, put it to my forehead, and cocked the trigger. I saw the bullets in the barrel and wet myself, afraid she'd actually fire the gun. The look on her face was like she was possessed by the devil. She said, 'if I see you around that girl ever again I will kill her first then you. Do you understand?' I shook my head and she lowered the gun only to place it in my ear. I cried, 'please, Mom, don't do it. I promise I'll never see her again'. There was no way I'd let her harm my one true love. I cried myself to sleep knowing that to even glance at Hannah could cause her harm.

The next entry read...

I insisted on leaving first thing. I didn't want to chance that Hannah would drop by. That terrified me. I wouldn't let my mother come with us to WTS because I wanted to tell my dad what she'd said and done. He was in one of his quiet moods and anytime I started to talk he'd shush me. I have to protect Hannah in any way I can. At least I know she will be safe at Tech. Maybe we can find a way to be together after mother settles down. How would she know? I started to write Hannah a letter explaining everything but stopped. My mother scares me and if she says she'll know, I half believe her. I cannot take the chance of Hannah losing her life.

"All this time I was hating her, not knowing that she was protecting me. Why didn't she just tell me?" Her eyes tracked to the journal. *I cannot take the chance of Hannah losing her life.*

Hannah took the note Charlie sent her via Nelly and opened it. With her thumbs, she punched in 8889760445 and waited nervously for it to ring.

"Hannah?" a breathless voice asked.

"Yes. We need to talk. Would you like that?"

"Yes, more than anything."

Hannah's phone beeped that she had another call. "Will you hold on for a minute? I have a call from my mama."

"Sure. Hey, why don't you call me back when you're finished talking to her."

"Okay, I'll call you right back." Hannah ended the call, then answered the other call. "Mama, is everything okay?"

"Yes, everything is perfect. We will be moving Daddy to Amarillo tomorrow afternoon."

"Oh, that is great news, Mama. When will you get there?"

"The plane will land around three. Can you meet me at the hospital?"

"How will you get to the hospital?"

"I'll take a cab if Mack can't get away from work."

"Okay, but let me know if anything changes."

"I will," Ada assured her.

"Is there anything you need?"

"No. I plan on going home with you to get us some clothes and wash what we have."

"When do you want to do that?"

"Day after we get Daddy settled at the hospital. You sound different. Is everything okay?"

"Everything is as it should be. I'll go tell Bo, we'll drive up there tomorrow."

"Okay, sweetie, I'll call you later to tell you his room number and all that kind of thing."

"Bye, Mama. Your news is terrific."

Hannah quickly tapped in Charlie's number and waited for her to answer. "My daddy is being moved to Amarillo tomorrow."

"That's fantastic news. Are you going there?"

"Probably. I'd like to see you before I go."

"How about I meet you at our place in say thirty minutes?"

"Sounds great to me. See you then, Charlie."

With a happy smile on her face, Hannah went to tell Bo her good news. Just as she was ready to go outside, her phone rang. "Hello."

"Hi Hannah, it's Sheriff Morgan. I have some news for you."

"About Mick?"

"Yep. You were right. She isn't Tom Hendricks' granddaughter. No relation at all, since he didn't have any heirs. Her real name is Bridgette Compton, and she's pulled off a long list of scams like she did here. We went to the house and were surprised that she was still there. Usually, in this type of crime, the perp makes some money and leaves. Apparently, she was waiting for a deal to come through on selling the house."

"That's great news, Lara. What happens to her now?"

"We've charged her, and she's in jail waiting for a bail hearing. I doubt she'll make bail."

"Am I in trouble? Did she try to implicate me?"

"She has an accomplice—a wife, she says— who gave up the whole story when confronted. Lara smiled. "No worries. There's nothing about this crime that concerns or incriminates you."

"Thank you for everything, Lara. I appreciate you taking me seriously."

"No problem." Lara let out a laugh. "Just doin' my duty, ma'am."

Hannah laughed. "Thanks again, Lara. Bye."

"Bye."

CHAPTER TWENTY☐ THREE

The closer Hannah got to the rock, their place, the more happiness surrounded her. After all the years, she knew the reason for Charlie's silence—she loved her so much that she was willing to let her go to keep her alive. It seemed preposterous to consider that Charlie's mother could do such a thing. Hannah felt there must be more to the story. In the distance, she could see Charlie sitting on the rock with her legs stretched out. It was just as she remembered seeing her the last time. She quickened her pace until she was standing on the rock.

"You came," Charlie said softly.

"Of course I came. I couldn't stay away." Hannah motioned to the rock. "Is it okay if I sit?"

"Yes."

The look in Charlie's eyes was the same one Hannah saw the last time they were together. They were filled with love and desire. "I've missed you almost more than I could bear." She hesitantly reached out and touched Charlie's hand. "I guess we have a few years to sort out."

"Yes, we do. Just so you know, my life was empty without you."

"Surely you had friends and went out."

"Friends, yes, but none that were close. As for going out," she shrugged, "no one I met could compare to my one true love. You." Charlie squeezed the hand holding hers. "What about you? Anyone other than Mick?"

Hannah took a deep breath while trying to decide whether to tell the truth or lie. There was no question truth was always the best thing to give. "Well, as you lived here, you know the pickin's aren't great for lesbians around here."

Charlie giggled. "It's amazing that we found each other."

"Yes, it was." Hannah moved closer to Charlie. "To tell you the truth, when Mick moved to town four or five months ago, I was drawn to her. Her grandpa had died and left her his house that was in need of a complete renovation. She was alone, and I felt sorry for her. I volunteered to help get the house fixed up so she could sell it."

"And?"

"I'm sure you remember that horrific day Mick came into Maudie's."

"Yes. I'm sure everyone in Maudie's spread the word about what happened."

Hannah could feel a blush burn her cheeks. "I'm sure they did. You should have seen how they all looked at me when I went back inside." Hannah looked away, then directly at Charlie. "She kept flirting with me, making all kinds of innuendos about what she'd like to do with me. Charlie, I was so lonely and lost that I did give in and kiss her a few times, but that was all." She caressed Charlie's cheek. "There was something off about her that I could never quite figure out. She was always vague about her life. I even caught her in a lie about where she grew up. When it came down to going further with the relationship, I just couldn't do it.

"Why?"

"I asked myself that question a lot, and I realized that I still loved you. I would have felt like I was betraying you if I did."

"Even though you thought I treated you horribly?"

"I was devastated when you walked away, Charlie. I never knew a heart could survive what I was going through. Yet there you were in my heart and thoughts. No matter how hard I tried, I couldn't stop thinking of you."

"I'm so sorry, Hannah. I didn't know what else to do. There was no doubt in my mind that my mother had hired someone to follow me. She would have killed you if I contacted you."

"Yeah, I know. I went by there to see why you didn't meet me. Your mother came to the door screaming at me for taking you down the path of repulsive behavior. She pulled a rifle on me, and when I was walking away, she shot at me."

"Oh my god." Charlie's hand went over her mouth. "Did you tell anyone?"

"I told your dad. I got the feeling he wasn't surprised. As far as I know, he didn't do anything about it."

"Yeah, any time she'd go off like that, he'd call me and we'd leave the house. On the days when I got home from school and he wasn't there, I had to find a place to hide in the house, if I saw she was going crazy again. Eventually, she found all my hiding places in the house, so I'd hide in the barn until I saw my dad come home."

Hannah pulled Charlie into her arms and held her close. "Why didn't you ever tell me then? We could have figured out something."

"I did. Remember, I told you she had problems." Charlie lifted a shoulder. "I should have been honest about just how bad it was."

"And I should have asked more questions and listened better."

"By the time we moved here, she was on lithium. That seemed to help. To tell you the truth, all I wanted to do was to be with you. You made me feel safe and protected."

Hannah kissed the top of Charlie's head. "Are we back together?"

"Yes. That's all that I ever wanted." Charlie look up and kissed Hannah. "But we have a lot of years to sort out before we can really move forward."

"And we will. I know you have a life in—"

"I never had more than half a life. Don't you get it? I was never complete."

"Neither was I."

"Now we are. Right?"

"Yes, and we will work it out. I promise. Now that we are together again, there is no way I will let you go. I always thought I should've gone to Canyon and hunted until I found you." Hannah grinned. "Actually, I did do that."

"Really?"

"Yep. Obviously, I didn't find you."

"Had you found me, I would've had to lie and tell you I didn't love you and to leave me alone. Writing that note to you was the hardest thing I ever did. That's why it took me so long to answer your letters."

"Bo is going to leave tomorrow morning so he can be in Amarillo when Mama's plane lands."

"Are you going with him?" Charlie asked.

"I was going to drive myself, so I could bring her back down here. But Mack is coming down to help out, so Mama and me will just come back with him. Then he will drive her back to Amarillo."

"That makes sense."

"Did I tell you that it gets really, really lonely at the house, especially at night? Wanna spend the night?"

"What about Oscar? Doesn't he stay in the house at night?

"Well yeah, he does. He's a good boy, and I'm glad that Nelly gave him to me. Will you come home with me?" Hannah asked.

"Spending the night with you sounds tempting." Charlie touched Hannah's arm. "I think we still have a lot to sort out before we take that step. Besides, isn't Bo staying there?"

"Yes he is, and you're right about taking our time. I don't like it, but it's what we *should* do."

"We need to get what's between us right. Even though you now know the truth, Hannah, aren't there unanswered questions and anger still lurking?"

Hannah nodded. "My head keeps saying *Danger, Danger Will Robinson.*" She put a hand over her heart. "In here, I know that isn't true. We need to get us back to where we were."

Charlie shook her head. "Don't you see, Hannah? We can never go back to where we were, but we can use our past to build a new future."

Hannah clutched Charlie to her and kissed her softly. "I like the sound of that."

"Trust in us, Hannah, and we will find our way back to the happiness we lost and so much more."

"I'm willing to try if you are." Another kiss reassured Hannah that they were indeed on the right path back to each other.

"Now, go get your things together so you and Bo can go see your daddy. Come back to me as soon as you can."

"Do you think you can stay at my house while I'm gone?" Hannah asked. "You know, to take care of Oscar. I can get Nelly to come stay too."

"Sure, I can do that."

"Okay, let me call Nelly. She has a key and has stayed here when I'd go to Houston."

"I will look forward to your return."

"I will be back. You can count on me."

"I know I can."

"Can you stay a while longer? Maybe we can go to my house and sit on the porch and just be together."

"I'd like that." Charlie grinned. "Race you." She stood and began to sprint away.

"Hey, no fair." A laughing Hannah took off after Charlie, heart soaring.

CHAPTER TWENTY⬜⬜OUR

Hannah walked into the hospital room and was surprised to see only her mama and daddy there. "I thought Bo would still be here," she said. "I only stopped to use the restroom."

"He said to tell you he'd be back in an hour. Patsy needed him for something." Ada smiled.

Hannah walked over to the bed and gave her father a kiss on the cheek, then did the same with her mother. "How are you feeling, Daddy?"

"Rough, but now that you're here, I'm feelin' better." Sam gave her what looked like a forced smile.

"Now, tell me the truth."

"The ride here took a lot out of me. Before we left, I was feelin' pretty good, but now not so much. The doc said it will pass."

"They did more blood tests when we got here. His white count is almost normal and if his labs are significantly better at his next appointment, he'll most likely get a light chemo round. In a week, he has an appointment with the transplant team." Ada looked at Sam lovingly. "Now that we have him here…" She wiped a tear from her eyes. "I know he's going to make it."

Hannah hugged her mother. "Yes, he will."

"Tell me about what's goin' on at home," Sam said in upbeat tone.

"Well, we are ready to harvest. The bolls look great. I think we'll get a premium price."

"On all the dry land too?"

"Yep. I've had a lot of help from Bo and Mack, along with our friends and neighbors. Everything is on schedule for harvestin'." Hannah looked at her daddy and saw that he'd fallen asleep. "Mama," she whispered. "Why don't you go back to Mack's house and take some time to yourself."

"I can't leave him."

"Daddy won't be alone. I'll be with him."

Ada looked at her and smiled. "I'm so glad you're here. Bo said you had some shopping to do."

"I want to find something for Nelly, for taking care of things at home when I've had to leave."

"You do know you don't need to get her anything."

Hannah smiled. "I know she has a sweet tooth for dark chocolate, so I want to get that for her."

"She'll love it." Ada patted her hand. "I'm glad you're here."

†

"He's getting his color back." Hannah was spending most of her time at the hospital.

"He looks better than he has since this all started. The doctors want us to join them this afternoon for a consultation. Will you be there, Hannah?"

"Of course. I wouldn't miss it."

The whole family stood around Sam's bed, waiting for the oncologist, Dr. Russell, to join them. A tall, kind-looking woman entered the room.

"Good morning," Dr. Russell said while walking to Sam's bed. "How are you feeling today, Mr. Garvin?"

"I'm feelin' better than when I first got here."

"Good. Is this your family?"

"Yes, ma'am."

Dr. Russell shook everyone's hand. "I'm glad you are all here. Considering all that is going on with Sam, he is doing remarkably well."

"What's next?" Ada asked.

"Well, he is going to have another round of chemo today. That will maintain his remission. The transplant team is working to identify a matched donor or a close familial match. I understand each of you have done the cheek swab to see if you are a possible donor. Once we release Sam, he needs to stay close by."

"We have an in-law suite, which would be perfect," Mack said.

Hannah could see the disappointment on her daddy's face. She knew he wanted to go home where his heart was. "Daddy, once you beat this thing, you can go back home." She looked at the doctor. "Right, Dr. Russell?"

"Yes. Once the stem cell transplant is done and his numbers settle, he can go home. But he will need regular checkups."

"Alrighty then, let's git this done so I can go home." Sam's attitude made everyone in the room smile.

†

With Mack driving, Hannah and her mother traveled south on highway sixty toward the farm. They had said their good-byes to everyone. They were going home to gather everything her parents would need for their extended stay in Amarillo. The plan was that Ada would go back with Mack and use one of his vehicles to travel back and forth to the hospital.

Hannah called Charlie when they stopped for a bathroom break. "Hey, I'm on my way back."

"Great. I can't wait to see you and can get it all straightened out so we can get back together for good. How about I make dinner for us?"

"As tempting as that sounds, Charlie, my mama and Mack are with me."

"I know, silly. You told me that they were coming back with you before you left."

Hannah let out a laugh. "You're right. So much has gone on, my mind gets muddled. Mama needs to get clothes and things to take back."

"I'll go over to your house and make dinner for everyone, if that's okay."

"That would be great." Hannah saw her mama coming toward the car. "Okay, we'll be on our way as soon as Mack comes back. I'll see in you in about an hour or so."

"Perfect. See you soon."

Hannah could hear the joy in Charlie's voice, and it made her heart sing. "Yes you will."

"Who were you talking to?" Ada asked when she got in the car. "Was it about Daddy?"

"No, it was Charlie.

"Charlie? Are you two back together?" Ada's smile was broad. "I'm sorry, I have been so preoccupied with Daddy that I haven't asked you what's happening with you. She's back with you and that's wonderful."

"Mama, we aren't back together just yet. We're just getting to know each other again."

"Amen. It's a start, and that is all that matters." Ada reached over and patted Hannah's hand. "I'm happy for you."

"Thanks, Mama. Here comes Mack, so we can get going."

The rest of the drive was in relative silence. The radio played softly in the background. When Mack guided his car down the dirt road toward the farm, Hannah's heart rate increased at the sight of Charlie's truck.

†

The screen door opened wide, and Charlie was standing there holding it open. "You made it. Supper should be ready in about an hour and a half. I just put it in the oven."

"Charlie, it's so wonderful to see you. I'm so sorry that you lost your mother. She was always kind to me." Ada gave her a hug.

"Thank you, Mrs. Garvin. I hope you like lasagna."

"I love it. Did you make it?"

"Yes."

"So do I." Mack walked through the front room, as he carried the suitcases inside.

Hannah watched the interactions among everyone, until Charlie's eyes captured her own. "Lasagna sounds like a lot of work," she said, not letting the connection go. She stepped forward and hugged Charlie. "Thank you," she whispered.

"It wasn't all that much work. I was glad to do that for you all."

"You're joining us aren't you, Charlie?" Ada asked.

"I wasn't planning on it. I figured you, Mack, and Hannah had a lot to do without me being in the way."

"Nonsense," Ada said firmly. "You are part of this family and should sit with us."

"Are you sure?"

Ada nodded.

"Then I'll stay."

"Good. I need the bathroom." Ada turned and walked away.

Charlie moved so she was in front of Hannah. "Are you sure you want me to stay?"

Hannah grinned and pulled Charlie to her. "More than you know." They kissed, then pulled apart when they heard Ada and Mack coming. "Later." Hannah winked.

"Mama, I'm going to go look over the cotton. I'll be back in about an hour. You coming with me, Mack?"

"Right behind you. Do I get a Gator of my own?"

Hannah laughed. "No, but you can drive."

"Okay." Ada kissed her daughter's cheek. Once the door slammed behind Hannah she turned to Charlie. "Are you anxious to get back to Canyon and your job?"

"No." Charlie shook her head. "I've taken leave for the rest of the school year."

"Why? What's here for you?"

"Hannah." Charlie put a hand over her heart. "She has always been my true north."

"You had no contact with her for all these years, so how on earth can you say that? Do you have any idea how devastated she's been since you left?" Ada was having trouble keeping her voice level. "There was no consoling her and believe me, I tried."

"Mrs. Garvin, I take it that Hannah hasn't shared why I had no contact for so long," Charlie said softly.

"When it comes to you, Charlene, she says very little. There were times when I just held her while she cried." Ada lifted a shoulder. "Occasionally she would mention you, but that was rare."

"I felt the same way every day." Charlie bent her neck and shook her head. "There was no way I could contact her. No way."

"Then tell me why you decided to come back into her life now, because when you leave, I will be the one to pick up the pieces again." Ada couldn't stop her anger.

"My mother threatened to kill her," Charlie whispered.

"What? I can't believe that! Your mother was the sweetest woman I've ever known."

"My mother was a paranoid schizophrenic, and my family were all experts in keeping it hidden. As long as she was on her medications, she was stable for a while. We never knew when she'd go off them, until she began telling us to turn off the television because the people in there were spying on us. She threatened to kill Hannah, because she saw us kissing. I took her threat seriously."

"I had no idea." Ada took a step and pulled Charlie into a hug. "You could have told me."

"No, I couldn't tell anyone. I knew she would follow through with her threat, and I couldn't risk your daughter's life."

Ada let go and wiped her tears away, noticing that Charlie was crying too. "Come on, I can smell the lasagna. We should check it out."

"Okay, but I don't think it's ready yet. I figured we'd eat at six."

"Would you like me to make a salad?"

"That would be perfect."

CHAPTER TWENTY☐ ☐IVE

Hannah stood on the small patch of grass in front of the house. She waved good-bye to her mother, then wrapped her arm around Charlie's waist and sighed. "Looks like I will be working this place by myself with no end in sight."

"I thought you had other farmers helping you."

"That all stopped a month ago. Right now, every farmer needs to be on their own farm. It's pickin' time."

"My dad never picked the cotton by hand. He used a cotton stripper."

Hannah laughed. "Pickin' time is a term Daddy used to let us know we were going to be busy. I do remember, at a young age, that all us kids had sacks over our shoulders and picked the cotton. Daddy said it wouldn't hurt us to know how he did it."

"You miss him, don't you?" Charlie hugged her.

"Yeah, I do." Hannah breathed in the scent of Charlie's hair, feeling her body relax. "Running this place by myself is overwhelming. I don't know if I can do it."

Charlie took a step back and looked at her. "You can set your mind to do anything you want to. There's always a way, Hannah." Charlie smiled. "Besides, you won't be doing all the work alone." She grinned. "You have me."

"You? What about your job? Your life in Canyon?"

"A few days ago, I resigned from my teaching position. All I need to do is clear out my apartment, then I'm here to stay."

Hannah couldn't believe her ears. "You did that?"

"Yes." Charlie grinned.

"But we haven't talked yet. What if—" A finger was placed over her lips.

"There is no doubt in my mind that my feelings for you haven't changed. There is nothing you can do to alter that. I'd rather be close to you with hope in my heart than miles away aching for you. The question is, how do you feel? Can you forgive me?"

"I'm speechless. Now that I know the why, I forgive you. I want to explore a life with you."

"Then come with me to Canyon. Help me clean out the apartment and settle things there."

"When do you want to go?"

"Tomorrow."

"Okay. Let me call Nelly to see if she'll come over and check on the house and Oscar while we're away."

†

The key clicked, and Charlie opened the door to her apartment. "Come on in and take a look at what I have to move. The place came furnished, so I don't have any bulky items. Mainly boxes and not a lot of them."

"If that pile of boxes is all you have, then we might need to get more." Hannah looked around the small apartment. She gasped. One wall was filled with pictures of her and Charlie over the years before Charlie left. "Charlie," she whispered. An arm went around her shoulders and squeezed.

"You were always with me and in my heart." Charlie took her hand. "Come."

Hannah went with Charlie into the bedroom. She thought she'd swallowed her heart. The bedside stand held a special photo of them together. Another sat on the dresser. "Oh my god, I can't believe I ever doubted you."

"How could you have known, Hannah?"

"I couldn't." Hannah looked around the room. "Have you been back here since your mother passed?"

"No, why would I?" Charlie gave her a quizzical look.

Hannah ran a finger over an end table and then held it up. "There's no dust."

"What are you saying?"

"Nothing." Hannah averted her gaze.

"Tell me the truth. If we are going to be an us again, you need to be honest with me."

"It's been weeks since your mother passed. Why isn't there dust?"

Charlie flopped down in a chair. "Do you think I came back and put the pictures up so you'd think I was true to you?"

Hannah shrugged and could feel her face heat from her blush. "I don't know what I think." She looked down at her shoes. "My heart tells me one thing, and my head something different. I want this to work, Charlie, I really do."

"Then let it happen. Trust me."

"I want to."

"Do you really trust me? Because it sure doesn't sound like it."

Hannah closed her eyes and shook her head.

"Hannah, you're a silly goose. I have someone come in to clean every other week. I called Maria three days ago. I told her I'd be moving and the place needed cleaning. She was here this morning."

"What a fool I am." Hannah buried her face in her hands and shook her head. "Can you ever forgive me?"

Charlie lifted Hannah's chin and smiled. "If you will forgive me for leaving."

†

The boxes were filled and the few items of furniture that Charlie had were all waiting by the door. Bo had offered to help load Hannah's pickup.

"When did Bo say he'd be here?" Charlie asked.

"In about a half hour. Did you want to start now?"

"Not what I had in mind." Charlie grinned and wrapped Hannah in her arms. "I was hoping we could have some cuddle time."

Hannah ran her finger across Charlie's hand. "After all the emotions earlier, I think that is exactly what we need." Her lips captured Charlie's, and soon her tongue was running over them seeking more. Charlie moaned into Hannah's mouth as she sucked her tongue. The long and passionate kiss was full of promise and reestablished their bond. A knock at the door had them both exhaling.

"Damn, he's never been on time in his life, and today he chooses to be early." Hannah opened the door and her mouth fell open. "You both came?"

"Bo here kept harassing me until I finally took the rest of the day off to help."

Hannah smiled. "Come on in."

"Hey, Charlie, it's good to see you again." Mack pulled her in for a hug.

"You too."

"I'm glad you're back together," Bo whispered when he hugged Charlie.

"Me, too."

"Okay, let's get this show on the road," Bo said. "Patsy is making us supper. Mama will be there, and if they can swing it, Daddy might come too."

"Sounds good to me." Hannah put her arm around Charlie. "We've got all the boxes packed and the few items of furniture Charlie has are ready to go too. Once they're in the truck we'll be on our way."

"I brought a dolly. Let me go get it." Bo picked up a box. "You three get a box each and come on." Bo walked out of the apartment with the others close behind.

†

Bo's house was a ruckus affair, with kids running around and yelling. Hannah shook her head and gave Bo's wife a hug. "Patsy, this is my girlfriend, Charlene."

"Nice to meet you, Charlene. Welcome to our home."

"It's good to finally meet you, Patsy. Please call me Charlie, everyone does. You have a fantastic home."

"Thank you. It's little bit harried right now, but I've fed the kids. We'll kick them out to the backyard and the trampoline while we eat. Right now, we're waiting for Ada to arrive."

"Charlie, this is my other sister-in-law, Lucy."

"Pleased to meet you, Charlie."

"Likewise, Lucy."

"I'm here at last," Ada called from the door. "I hope I haven't held you all up."

"Not at all. Hannah and Charlie just arrived," Patsy said.

"Mama, you're here." Hannah hurried over to her.

Ada gave Hannah a hug and held on to her a bit longer than necessary. "I'm so glad you're here."

"How's Daddy doing?"

"The chemo gave him a urinary infection, so he is semi-isolated. I'm afraid you won't be able to go into his room."

"That's not a problem. Before we go back, Charlie and I will stop by even if we have to look at him through a window and wave."

"He will like that."

CHAPTER TWENTY☐☐IX

Hannah pulled the pickup into the barn.

"Why are you parking in here? Where's Oscar?"

"Nelly has him."

"I thought you were taking me to my father's house."

"It's too late to unload the truck tonight. Your dad is probably already in bed. Besides, didn't you tell me he was going to lease his land and move to Silverton?"

"Yeah, but—

"Charlie." Hannah cupped her cheek. "You've quit your job, moved out of your apartment, and your dad is moving. You can stay here forever if you want."

"What happens when your folks come back?"

"We will figure that out when that time comes, if...and it's a big if...they come back at all." Hannah wiped a hand over her face. "I do know that I can't work this place by myself. I'm gonna need to find somebody—"

Charlie held a finger over Hannah's lips. "You don't have to. If you're hiring, I'm applying."

Hannah's eyes opened wide. "Really?"

"Of course, silly. I do know my way around a cotton farm." Charlie took Hannah's hand. "And you, my love."

Overwhelmed by the emotion the moment caused, Hannah was shaking. "It's a deal then. I'm hiring you." She didn't even try to stop the broad smile she knew covered her face. She pulled Charlie close.

Charlie gave her a peck on the cheek and grinned. "So, where am I going to sleep tonight? With you?"

"That sounds tempting. Are you sure? There are other bedrooms you can sleep in."

"If I promise not to do anything you don't want me to, can I sleep with you? I want to feel your arms around me when I go to sleep. I can't tell you the number of times I pretended you were holding me. It was the only time I felt safe."

"Then I guess we'd better get our bags inside."

Charlie yawned. "It has been a long day."

Hannah dropped both backpacks on her bedroom floor. "I think the best I can do for tonight is go to the bathroom and brush my teeth." She scratched her head. "I'm exhausted. What about you?"

"I'm with you, babe. All I want to do is pull the covers up and go to sleep in your arms."

"Let's take the day tomorrow and see if we can come up with a plan for our future together."

"I'd like that, Hannah. Trust me, if I wasn't so tired right now, I'd be tempted to undress you and have my way with you." Charlie grinned. "Although—"

"No, Charlie. No."

Charlie put her arms around Hannah and pulled her close. "First we kiss." She licked her lips and kissed Hannah. "Then, I undress you." She began unbuttoning the shirt, until Hannah stopped her.

"I think I'd better find somewhere else to sleep."

"No. Please don't. I promise to be good."

Hannah raised her eyebrows and stepped backward. "Right now, my body is screaming, 'Undress her and make love.' I want to get to know who you've become, Charlie, and not give in to my body. Can you understand that?"

"Of course I can. We're in this together."

"I think we're on the road to a great romance." Hannah added. "I do love you so much, Charlie."

"As I do you. I also know that every relationship, and I mean every single one, not just the romantic kind, has its ups and downs. If we keep that in mind, I think we can face anything that comes our way." Charlie held out her hand. "Come on, let's go to bed. I promise, all I'll do is hold you."

Hannah took Charlie's hand and could feel the connection they'd had ever since they first met. "I trust you always." She wiggled her eyebrows. "I think that by the time we get in the bedroom we won't be sleeping right away."

"I like the sound of that." Charlie took her hand and walked quickly toward the bedroom.

†

"Yoo-hoo are you decent?" a voice called out.

"Nelly?" Hannah got out of bed pulled on a shirt and jeans. When she opened the bedroom door, Oscar came bounding in and began jumping on her. "Oscar, no. Go find Nelly."

"What's going on," a craggy voiced Charlie asked.

"Go back to sleep. It's Nelly. She's probably here for the eggs."

Charlie sat up in the bed and stretched her arms high. "That was nice."

"What? Nelly getting the eggs?"

"No, silly. Sleeping with you spooning me."

"Hannah, is that you?" Nelly called.

"Yes, I'll be right there."

"Okay, I'll start the coffee."

"Great." Hannah turned to Charlie. "Go back to sleep. It's still early."

"No, I'll be down in a few minutes."

Hannah walked into the kitchen. Nelly was sitting at the table with what looked like a satisfied grin. "I didn't think this was your egg day."

"It isn't, but Oscar said he was ready to come home. What could I do but bring him here?"

Hannah shook her head. "Ah."

"Good morning, Nelly. How've you been?" Charlie gave the older woman a bright smile, and Nelly nodded in her direction.

"I've been good, and I can tell by that smile you are even better than that."

"Oh, that is true." Charlie walked over to Hannah and took her hand. "All the planets are aligned now."

Nelly grinned. "I'm glad to hear that. Now, down to business."

Hannah frowned. "Has something happened?"

"Well, yes and no. I spoke with your mama last night, Hannah. She is concerned about you tryin' to run this place alone."

"She won't be alone," Charlie blurted, "I'm going to help her."

"I'll be okay, Nelly. We'll be okay working the place together."

"I'm sure you will, but you also realize there will be times when two won't be enough."

"And I will find someone to help. That's what Daddy and I did in the past."

"Okay. My nephew, Braydon, is coming to live with me and help around the place. He's a good worker, and I'm sure he will help you out when you need him."

"Okay, I'll keep that in mind." Hannah was getting upset. She'd worked the farm all her life and knew what to do. "You do know, Nelly, this isn't my first rodeo."

"I know. I also know that your daddy is worried about you doin' this alone. He wanted to know if you'd made arrangements for the cotton pickers."

"I got my name on the list a month ago. I believe we are the first to be done." Hannah blew out a breath. "I'll call him later and let him know that Charlie is here to help me."

"I'm sure he'll rest easier. Your mama said they're lifting the isolation tomorrow. She sounds worn out. I offered to go take her place, so she can rest for a few days—"

"And she refused."

Nelly nodded.

"I've offered the same thing many times, and she always says no. The few times she came back here, she finally relaxed. I could see her stiffen when she'd go back."

"It's hard on everyone, sweetheart." Charlie put her arm around Hannah. "I remember the same thing happening when my grandma had cancer."

"Well, enough sad talk. Why don't you two sit at the table and let me make you breakfast?"

"As long as it is pancakes, I'm in." Hannah laughed. "I've had more eggs since I've been here alone than I can count."

All the women laughed, and Nelly set about making pancakes.

While they were eating breakfast, the house phone rang and Hannah answered it. "Hello... Okay, that will work... What time?... All right, see you then." She hung up the phone and turned to Charlie and Nelly. "They're going to start harvesting in an hour. They're waiting for the last harvester to arrive." Hannah wiped a hand over her face. "This is something that Daddy did and never included me. Hell, I haven't a clue how much it will cost. I can't call him. That will just get him all upset, and he doesn't need that right now."

"Call your mama," Charlie said. "I bet she will know."

"I guess. But what if she doesn't? What am I going to do?"

"Stop working yourself up," Nelly said. "Let me tell you about costing and what happens next. I learned all about it from my late husband."

"Thanks, Nelly, I'd really appreciate that."

"You'll pay whatever the going rate is per pound." Nelly pursed her lips. "Does your daddy have an office or a filing cabinet where he keeps his papers?"

"Yes. He set up a little office for himself in the barn."

"Well then, let's go look and see what he paid last year."

Charlie headed for the door. "Come on, let's go find out."

†

Early that night, Hannah flopped down on the bed and yawned. "What a day," she said. "Who would have thought, when we got up this morning, so much would happen."

"We worked well together," Charlie said as she sat on the edge of the bed.

Hannah reached out and rubbed Charlie's back. "I just don't know if we can run this place by ourselves."

"Of course we can." Charlie kissed Hannah's cheek. "Together, we are unstoppable."

"That we are." Hannah rubbed her palm over her mouth, then gave Charlie a serious look. "You make me a better person. I was nothing without you in my life. When you were gone, I was lost. I always tried to put on my happy face around everyone, even though I was slowly dying inside. With you here, my heart is full of love, and I know that our future is limitless."

"Hannah, that first day when I was sitting on that rock before you got there, I was so angry about moving. I liked where we were. We had to leave because of my mother. She accused a neighbor lady of trying to seduce my dad. The neighbor had a restraining order filed against her. That led to a whole lot of legal stuff, and my dad felt he had only one choice, to move. I hated her for that."

"Why didn't you ever tell me about her? All you ever said was she had spells."

"I should have. At first, I was embarrassed. After I got to know you, I knew it wouldn't make any difference."

Hannah gave her a puzzled expression.

"When I first looked up and saw this beautiful girl coming my way and smiling at me, my heart grew wings. I felt the earth shift, and I knew I'd found my *one*. Over time, I learned that you loved me no matter what, and it had nothing to do with my mother."

Hannah snapped her fingers. "Just like that?"

"Yes, it was truly amazing. I was completely taken by you."

Hannah gathered Charlie in her arms. "You were my first love. My last love. My always love."

"I was devastated when I left. I cried all the way to Canyon and for days after I got there." Charlie laughed. "My roommate thought I was homesick. Little did she know. I cried every night for months, trying to work up the courage to tell you why I left. Then I got a letter from my mother. She told me she'd seen you in town with your mother and wished she had her gun. She wanted to kill you both. She sent letters describing how she'd kill you. A few times, she made references to what I was doing at school. I knew that either she'd hired someone, or she was at my school watching me." Charlie sucked in a breath. "It terrified me."

"That's over now, Charlie. You're safe. We will be together for always, and that is a promise."

"What will we do when your parents come back? Will we still stay in the same bedroom?"

"We will always be together. My mama and brothers know about us. I suspect my daddy does too, or at least he suspects." Hannah leaned in and kissed Charlie softly. Passion kindled and flamed.

Charlie pulled back and smiled. "Is this okay?" she asked, as she unsnapped the first pearl inlay of Hannah's shirt.

"Yes." Hannah put her hands on either side of Charlie's midsection and pushed her shirt up. "Is this okay?"

"Oh, most definitely." Soon they were naked and lying together face to face. They touched and explored the bodies that each had longed for over the years.

Sated and giddy, Hannah said, "Memory never forgets. The way you touched me just now was just like the memory of the first time we made love."

"I love you, Hannah. I always have. You are my first and last love."

"I love you too, Charlie. I always have and always will. I tried to find a way not to love you, but I never could."

Charlie

EPILOGUE

_____

Spring had arrived, and Hannah watched Charlie guide the tractor and moldboard plow over the last of the fields. For someone who had never driven a tractor, Charlie had taken to it like a duck to water. Pride filled Hannah's heart, for Charlie had stepped up and effortlessly become a true partner in running the farm. Life was good, and she felt blessed to have so much love in her life.

Hannah and Charlie maneuvered their tractors close to the barn, where they would detach the plows. Hannah climbed down, then went to Charlie and lifted her off the tractor. "Let's get these cleaned up, and I'll take you to town for dinner."

"That sounds perfect." Charlie kissed her lover. "Where are you taking me?"

Hannah laughed. "Rosie's is the only place open tonight." She began sweeping the dirt off the plow. "What do you think about inviting everyone here for Easter?" Hannah grinned. "We have the eggs."

"Sounds great to me. Maybe we can have it on Saturday instead of Sunday? That way we will have more time, and no one will feel pressured to leave early."

"That's a great idea. Maybe they can all stay over, and we can go to church as one big family."

Charlie sighed. "Hopefully, we won't have a repeat of last Christmas at my dad's house."

"No, we won't." Hannah remembered the past Christmas.

Hannah pulled the pickup in the driveway of Bobby Gaines' home in Abilene and saw him sitting on the porch. He stood and smiled broadly, as he walked toward the truck.

Hi, Dad." Charlie hugged him.

"It's good to see you, Mr. Gaines." Hannah held out her hand and he took it.

"I'm glad you two got here safe."

"No worries about that. Hannah is an excellent driver." Charlie took Hannah's hand and squeezed it. "When will Junior, Vera, and the kids get here?"

"Not for a while yet. Let me help you with your bags."

Once inside the house, Hannah noticed that Bobby left their bags by the door. She pointed at them. "Do you want me to put those somewhere?"

His eyes darted around the room. "In the spare bedroom. It's down the hall on the left."

"Let me help you," Charlie said. She looked at her father and smiled. "Thank you for inviting us. The house looks festive. You did a great job."

"Thank you, sweetheart. I wanted it to be nice for you and your brother"—he shrugged—"for the first Christmas without your mother."

Charlie hugged her dad again. "We will have a wonderful time."

They had been at the house for about an hour, when a grey Beemer pulled into the driveway. "Looks like your brother is here," Bobby said.

Hannah noticed his hand shook as he opened the door.

Junior came in the room, followed by his wife and two kids. Bobby bent down and held his arms out to the children. Charlie had told Hannah that the relationship with her brother had always been contentious. When she saw Junior give his sister a hug, she smiled. *Everything must have changed.*

"What is *she* doing here?" Junior's eyes fixed on Hannah and she shivered.

"She came with me." Charlie stepped away from her brother.

"Are you going back today?" Junior demanded.

Charlie stood beside Hannah and shook her head.

"Dad only has two bedrooms. Which one of you is going to be sleeping on the couch?"

"Junior, let it go," Bobby implored. "It's Christmas. A time of love and happiness."

Junior clenched his teeth and snarled. "I want nothing to do with homo*sex*uals. They are the devil's seed." He pointed at Hannah and Charlie. "I will not subject my wife and children to their deviance. Either they go, or we do."

Charlie grabbed Hannah's hand. "I knew this was a bad idea, but I held out hope that we could all get along." She swiped at the tears on her cheeks. "We will leave."

"I'll get our bags," Hannah said softly.

"No," Bobby said. "Please don't go," he begged. "I've looked forward to you being here ever since I moved here. You're my baby girl."

"And there we have it. Daddy's little girl who always gets everything," Junior spat. "Vera, get the kids ready. We're leaving."

Hannah could see the devastation on Bobby's face, as he hugged his grandson close. "Why are you doing this to your father?" she asked Junior.

"He knows how I feel about your kind, and he invited you here to rub it in my face." He pointed at Charlie. "She's always been his favorite. I was nothing to him or our mother." He pulled the little boy away from his grandfather. "Let's go."

Once the door slammed behind her brother, Charlie went to her father and hugged him. "Can we stay?"

"Of course you can." Bobby shook his head. "He's more like his mother than he knows. His heart is full of hate."

"I see eggnog on the counter. Who wants some?" Hannah asked, trying to lift the mood.

"I'd like some. What about you, Dad?"

"Sounds good. How about some whiskey in it?"

"You got it." Hannah saw the sadness on Charlie's face and went to give her a hug. "We'll work it out," she whispered.

"Thank you for being here with me."

Hannah remembered holding Charlie while she cried. She knew that wouldn't happen with their upcoming Easter event. Her family would fill this holiday with acceptance and love. They certainly wouldn't invite Junior, but Charlie's dad was invited. He'd said he would come. Everyone in her family knew she and Charlie were a couple. As far as Hannah knew, they were all accepting of the relationship.

†

"Do you think we have enough eggs?" Nelly asked. "How many kiddos will be here?"

"Not sure, Nelly. Bo has three and Mack four. I think that Patsy's sister and her family are coming too." Hannah put a sticker on the last colored egg. "I think we have six dozen eggs, so that should be enough."

Charlie came into the kitchen with a box full of Easter baskets. "We need to put grass in these, along with the candy."

"On it." Hannah kissed Charlie's cheek.

Ada came into the kitchen and smiled. "I'm so glad to be home again. I put the ham in the oven and made the scalloped potatoes. What else do you need me to do?"

"Mama, there's a list on the table. I think we've done most of it, but I keep having a nagging feeling we've forgotten something." Hannah finished putting the grass in the baskets. "When Bo and Mack get here, they can set up the tables and chairs."

"I'm glad the weather is cooperating. We can have our Easter feast outside," Charlie added.

"Is your dad coming, Charlie?" Nelly asked.

"He said he would be here." Charlie looked at Hannah, who squeezed her arm. "I'm looking forward to seeing him. I haven't seen him since last Christmas. I spoke to him a few days ago, and he said he was coming."

The back door slammed shut, and they all looked to see who was coming in.

"Girly, I've been lookin' around. You and Charlie have done a good job."

Hannah hugged her father close. "We couldn't have done it without you. Every time I'd go out to work and got stuck, I'd say to myself 'What would Daddy do?' You gave me the solutions."

Sam hugged her close. "I was waitin' for supper to say this," he sucked in a breath. "It looks like we'll be stayin' in Amarillo for quite a while longer."

"I thought the bone marrow transplant worked." Hannah whispered.

"It did, girly. I just need to be close to the doctors for a while longer than we thought."

"But you will be back. Right?"

"As soon as I can."

Hannah looked around the kitchen and noticed they were alone. "I love you, Daddy. Please get better. I need you here."

Sam kissed her cheek and hugged her close. "I'm workin' on it, girly."

Outside, Hannah could hear car doors closing and the sounds of excited children. "Time for the circus to begin," she said with a laugh.

"Wouldn't have it any other way," Sam said as he let her go.

†

After the meal, the adults sat around the table, while the kids were running around and laughing.

"Thank you for today," Hannah said to everyone. She squeezed Charlie's hand. "We are especially happy that Daddy was able to join us, along with Charlie's dad. We are now a complete family."

"You're welcome, my love. It's good to see everyone smiling and happy."

"The day isn't over yet." Hannah grinned as she stood. "Can I have everyone's attention?"

Everyone at the table stopped talking and looked at Hannah.

"I want to thank all of you for coming and proving again that family is everything." She looked at Charlie. "Charlie is the newest member of our family." She waved her hand over the surroundings. "None of this would have happened without her." Hannah dropped to a knee. "Charlene Gaines, will you do me the honor of marrying me?"

Charlie put a hand over her mouth. "Yes, yes I will."

Everyone around the table erupted in applause and well wishes. Hannah took Charlie in her arms. "I love you now and forever." She held her hand out, admiring her ring when an arm went around her shoulders.

"Congratulations, sweetheart." Bobby Gaines engulfed his daughter in his arms. "I am so happy for you."

†

The night was balmy. A few fireflies lifted from the ground to flash and dance, while the cacophony of crickets and cicadas accompanied the random howl of a coyote. Hannah Garvin sat on the wraparound porch, in the rocker that once belonged to her great-grandfather. It was at this time, in the dark of night, when she was acutely aware of the distinct possibility that she would be the last link of her once prominent and proud family, farming in the panhandle of Texas. As she slowly rocked, the vision of her girlhood best friend, Charlie, came to mind. She always did. Charlie was her one true friend, who knew her inside and out and loved her anyway. At least, that's what she'd thought until Charlie disappeared without a word. Her thoughts began to traverse memories of their times together, just as the spring on the screen door screeched. Hannah looked up and smiled. Charlie carried out plastic tumblers of iced tea.

"Hey, I was just thinking about you."

"Good things I hope."

"Always. I was wondering if we should set the date for our wedding."

Charlie beckoned Hannah over to the swing, and they snuggled close. "And, I was wondering how many kids we'd have."

"Wedding first, then kids."

Consumed by an overwhelming need, Hannah pulled Charlie to her and kissed her passionately. "Forever, I will be yours."

"And I yours," Charlie said before they kissed again.

"I think it's bedtime, don't you?"

Charlie took her hand. "We have our whole lives ahead of us."

ABOUT THE AUTHOR

ERIN O' REILLY

When Erin isn't writing she is bird watching or rock hunting. Over the last fifteen years of writing novels she has published twenty-four books, some in collaboration with JM Dragon. Her focus as a writer is to develop strong characters that make a dramatic impact on her storylines. Ten years ago, along with JM Dragon, she formed Affinity Rainbow Publications. She is the Technical Director and CEO of the publishing company.

Erin would love to hear from you at:
erinoreilly55@gmail.com

OTHER A□□INITY □OO□□

The Panty Thief by Annette Mori
Someone is stealing panties, but who? And why? Joey Hartford is a fourth-year medical student who insists she doesn't have time for a relationship. A new tenant in her apartment building is proving too tempting to ignore. Sabrina is in her final year of her doctoral program focused on completing her dissertation. Meeting Joey is dangerous for so many reasons. Add a suicidal ex-girlfriend who suddenly reappears in Sabrina's life and Joey's jealous friend-with-benefits, and things get complicated quickly.

Country Living by Jen Silver
Peri Sanderson achieves her dream of moving from London to a cottage in the English countryside with her wife, Karla. Peri sees their future as pastoral while chatting with the locals in a quaint village pub. Sexy urbanite, Karla, has other ideas. Secrets are everywhere. Peri quickly senses something not quite right among her rural neighbours and Karla.

Temptation, betrayal and intrigue combine to change the lives of both women beyond anything they could have imagined.

Before the Light by Samantha Hicks
One year after, her long-time partner Meredith's abduction, and their subsequent break-up, Kathleen Bowden-Scott's life is spiralling out of control. She meets Bethany Jones and despite an instant attraction Kathleen shies away. In this fast-paced, romantic suspense, lies are exposed and hearts unite as Kathleen and Beth fight for their future.

Wanted for Christmas by JM Dragon
Belle Farrow knew what she wanted for Christmas–work. She had little to offer but a minor degree in cookery and household management. Certainly not enough for a decent chef or housekeeper position. Then she saw an advert in the local newspaper. Wanted: Housekeeper/cook/nanny for the period of Christmas until the New Year. This is Christmas. Perhaps Santa reads the ad column too and pushes a little spirit of the season to that request.

Dreams in a Jar by JM Dragon
When you believe your life is a never-ending spiral of despair and the only personal joy you have is inside of a novel, would you grab a chance to hide away in the local bookstore and dream of adventures? Thea's life is about to embark on a journey she never envisioned when local bookstore owner, Marion, is taken ill. Her niece, Sheryl Appleby, takes over the reins and her presence provides Thea the courage to take a leap of faith. Can she embrace the butterfly effect, or are Thea's dreams bottled in a jar forever?

Pleasure Workers by Annette Mori
Alex Cortez is accomplished at two things, fixing broken
equipment and pleasuring women. She is happily doing both
at the Ranch in Nevada. Danna Nichols, newly widowed,
feels lost and alone. When her good friend Lindy invites her
to check out the newly established Trophy Wives Club, it
awakens dormant feelings and desires. An instant attraction
happens and the two form a bond under unlikely
circumstances. Will the challenges of their social status tear
them apart before they can enjoy the pleasures of their new
love?

The Trophy Wives Club by Ali Spooner
What happens when under-appreciated professional women
are offered their dream jobs? When one of Atlanta's elite
businesswomen and wife of a prominent judge sets her sights
on a goal, life begins to change for these women. Friendships
and romance bloom in a unique fitness club on the outskirts
of Atlanta, where more than a workout is offered.

Unknown Forces by Samantha Hicks
Jennifer Wilson spent the last seventeen years raising her
younger sister Kelsey after a boating accident killed their
parents. Riley hasn't had an easy life either and her
friendship with Kelsey is the only thing steadfast in her life.
When tragedy and secrets emerge, Jennifer and Riley must
learn to lean on each other. The growing attraction between
them only complicates matters. When events conspire to
keep them apart, will they trust the unknown forces that keep
pushing them together, or hide from their feelings forever?

<u>A Window to Love</u> by Annette Mori
Two life events, two paths colliding, two souls destined to meet. Mandie Carter lives an uninspired life. No passion, no romance, and just when she thought things couldn't get worse, life throws her a curve. Gail Forrester is barely hanging on. Buried under mountains of debt, only her much in demand architectural designs keep her afloat. Now, they must find a way forward together through what life and destiny has in store for them. Only then can they hope to step into that window to love.

<u>Free Spirit</u> by Erica Lawson
Priory McAllister has fought off boardroom sharks, handled high-pressure jobs, and thought she'd seen it all. She found her dream home and couldn't wait to move in. Unknown to Priory, two ghosts…Rhee and a mischievous Dylan…have inhabited the house since 1935. They have no intention of leaving. Jacey Ryder, Priory's long-suffering secretary, gets to play referee between her boss and a bossy ghost, as each side try to lay claim to the house. What can she do when an unstoppable force, (her boss) meets an immovable object, (the ghost) besides hope for a peaceful solution? They are like two peas in a pod—two *angry, stubborn* peas in a pod.

<u>Addicted to You</u> by Erin O'Reilly
Elin Prescot's dream to be a top fashion designer is finally within her reach—then Marissa Banks enters her life. Snared by her first taste of passion, Elin is consumed by desire for more. Her life spirals out of control until she meets Doctor Aimee Sullivan, who understands all too well what Elin is going through. Can Elin let Aimee into her heart? Or will her addiction keep her enthralled with Marissa? This story

explores first love, intense passion, manipulation of emotions, and the gentleness of real love and true romance.

At Last by JM Dragon
A perfume company in trouble, leading to a town in peril. Old Loves. Unrequited Loves. New passions. Can the reclusive Gene Desrosiers save her family company and the people she cares for, even though some are not aware of it yet? Will an ultimate sacrifice win the day, or will Grady end up a ghost town of unfulfilled lives? This love story will warm your heart.

Deuce by Jen Silver
When Jay Reid was in her twenties, she had it all. A professional tennis career, Charlotte, the love of her life and a new baby. Charlotte's research vessel, *RV Caspian*, was lost at sea, leaving Jay to raise their child alone. Rescued by a local fisherman, with no memory of her life before, she lives on the Faroe Islands as Katrin Nielsen. Seeing a beached seal one day triggers her memory. Twenty-three years is a long time. Is the love they once shared strong enough to be rekindled or have too many years passed eroding all hope of a happy ever after?

After Dark by Samantha Hicks
Can a love that starts out in terror be real or last? Meredith Ashcroft disappears on her way to a client meeting. Five months later, art gallery manager Stephanie Edwards is also held and tortured by the same sadistic man. Thrown together trying to overcome their shared ordeal, they find themselves falling in love. Is it true love or just an attachment to each other born out of fear for their lives?

<u>True North</u> by Ali Spooner
Cam's story continues as the Gator Girlz business continues to thrive under her leadership, but will self-doubt jeopardize her relationship when Bugsy reveals the family moonshine business to an unsuspecting Luce? Will a devastating injury to Sandy end her career as a gator hunter or will it open a door to love? Join the St. Angelo family for a third adventure to find out more about life, loving, and family in Bayou Country.

<u>The Dream Catcher</u> by Annette Mori
What if all your dreams—the good ones and the nightmares—came to life in the real world?
Heaven is a Dream Weaver, and that is her reality. When she wakes up, she never knows what will greet her or her best friend and roommate, Syl. It could be a sexy stripper or a monster from another dimension. When Syl suggests a Dream Catcher to help her control the dreams, Heaven is wary until she meets the alluring Maya. Between the government and the powerful Dream Catching sisters, time is running out for Heaven. She wonders who she can trust. Can this lovely Dream Catcher protect her or is Heaven truly on her own?

<u>Gator Girlz</u> by Ali Spooner
In the sequel to Diamond Dreams, Cam St. Angelo finished her freshman year on a high. Her softball career is on path. Everything seems to fall in place for Cam and Tab as the new school year and softball season take off. All too soon, unfortunate events at the home front force Cam to leave

college and her softball dreams behind. As always, it's family first.

The Tempest by JM Dragon
Doctor Alana Cameron has dedicated her life to working on the family legacy, a transportation device which will change the world for everyone, called Tempest. Tragedy has dogged the project over the years, causing military intervention. Super soldier Major Denise Tranter, who loyally defends Earth in any way possible, finds herself drawn into the Tempest program. Emotional bonding is not in her remit, although she finds herself inexplicably drawn to Alana.

Trusting Hearts by Samantha Hicks
When successful advertising executive Carrie-Ann Stedman is tasked to train a new hire, she is reluctant. She has never forgiven Holly Fletcher, the newbie, for stealing an important client away from her. Holly doesn't know what Carrie's problem with her is. When the two are thrown together, can they build a working relationship without business getting in the way of the growing attraction between them?

Free to Love by Ali Spooner and Annette Mori
Captain Hillary Blythe loves sailing the ocean. Her journeys along the Atlantic Coast and Caribbean to deliver goods contain many adventures. When she brings a small group of rescued Africans to the Methodist mission on Antigua, challenges to deeply ingrained beliefs arise when devoted Christian, Elizabeth Allen, is drawn to one of the women, Kia. Will Kia and Elizabeth be free to love among the harsh laws of the land and Elizabeth's struggles with her faith?

Kai's Heart by Renee MacKenzie
The time has come for the Resistance to take back control of New America from the Anointed tyrants. Growing up as the daughter of a Resistance Army General, Kai Brodie's focus is keenly on the upcoming Revolution. So how is it then that she can't take her eyes off the beautiful Anointed guard? Can Kai break free from tradition and find love in the arms of someone her upbringing tells her she should hate? Can she protect her love from those who hunt them? Will Kai and Rachel survive the battle over the fate of their beloved New America?

Diamond Dreams by Ali Spooner
Cameron St. Angelo dreams of playing softball in the College World Series. Earning a scholarship to play ball for her beloved LSU brings Cam one step closer to achieving this dream. When Cam arrives on campus, she joins a family of women who share her love of the sport, and she realizes there is room in her life for another love.

Unconventional Lovers by Annette Mori
Bri and Siera are young women with huge hearts and strong wills; they want nothing more than to find a peaceful and secure space to be themselves. But the world is a harsh place for anyone who is different. Bri's Aunt Olivia is a vet who channels her emotions into her work and her love of Bri. Siera has her Aunt Deb who adores her. Despite their individual battles against hurt, prejudice, and rejection, can these four women find love against the odds?

Affinity
Rainbow Publications

eBooks, Print, Free eBooks

Visit our website for more publications available online.

www.affinityrainbowpublications.com

Published by Affinity Rainbow Publications
A Division of Affinity eBook Press NZ LTD
Canterbury, New Zealand

Registered Company 2517228

www.ingramcontent.com/pod-product-compliance
Lightning Source LLC
Chambersburg PA
CBHW071141260626
47162CB00003B/873